SEVEN LIVES OF LIFE

SEVEN LIVES OF LIFE

SHANNEN DSOUZA

Anecdote
Publishing House
For the love of quality reading!

Anecdote
Publishing House
For the love of quality reading!

anecdotepublishinghouse.com
champreaders.com

Anecdote Publishing House
2nd Floor 2/15 Lane no. 2 Ansari Road, Daryaganj-110002
Email: info@anecdotepublishinghouse.com
Website: anecdotepublishinghouse.com

Published by Anecdote Publishing House

First Edition 2025
ISBN 978-81-973806-0-0
MRP ₹ 350

Book Promoted and Marketed by Champ Readers Pvt. Ltd.
Edited by Meraki
Cover design and Layout by Graphic Tailor
Printed by Thomson Press (India) Ltd, New Delhi

WARNING

This novel may contain sensitive content that could be distressing for some readers. Please be aware that the story may explore themes such as violence, mental health, substance abuse. If you have experienced trauma or are sensitive to these subjects, please proceed with caution.

CONTENTS

CHAPTER 1
THE BOOK

The alarm clock rang so loudly, causing me to wake up from my deep sleep. I rubbed my eyes slowly, one hand scratching my hair while the other one searching to put the alarm clock off. My eyes slowly adjusted to the bright yellow and blue colours in my room.

"I cannot wait to get my new phone," I murmured to myself.

Once I get my new phone, I'm going to set up soothing tunes of the ocean or the nature to nicely wake me up instead of this irritating one from the clock. This was nothing compared to my brother's – his alarm felt like some cat screeching at the top of its voice.

Thankfully, I will be up before his alarm would ring and would not have to listen to that wretched thing. I rested with my eyes closed for another five minutes, not getting the motivation to get out of the bed. I knew I would be late again if I didn't wake up in the next 5 minutes.

After doing a slow countdown starting from 5, I slowly opened one eye and saw Jason in deep sleep. Well, as long as he's having a nap, I too might relax for a bit.

But then I remembered that Jason takes so much of time in the bathroom god knows doing what and I didn't want to again spend the next ten minutes fighting with him on this. He would take up all of my time causing me to leave for school in a mess.

I felt Jason waking up next to me. I immediately got up, rushed to the bathroom. My hair was all frizzy again as I looked in the mirror. I had prominent dark circles under my eyes, which were a surprise, considering I had slept very well last night. My parents call me 'Sleeping Beauty' due to the amount of sleep that I get, but now due to the extra recitals that are going on, my best friend's crisis and also I am struggling in History, more so with the teacher than the subject which has added to my stress.

Plus Jason was getting more grumpier day by day. The last few weeks were a bit more tedious than usual, but judging by the looks of it, it was going to get even more worse for sure.

As I got out of the shower, Jason finally decided to wake up.

"Good morning, Jason," I said.

"Sure," he replied half in sleep and yawning his way into the bathroom.

If there was one person that I knew who could sleep better than me, it was this boy. He once slept for 19 hours straight after he had gotten back from a school trip. I thought he wasn't going to wake up at all!

I looked at the to-do list on the door of my wardrobe as I picked out my outfit, which was a perfect blend of a smart and pretty look, with a hint of casualness as well.

I rushed out and saw mom and dad eating breakfast. We have two rules at the dining table. First, always be grateful for your meal. Second, no gadgets on the table. We make a point to always sit at the dining table for food and would usually eat together. Honestly, I kind of like that as all of us eat together since we are busy all the time, especially during the weekdays and we would only have this common time to see each others' faces.

"So what plans for the day?" asked my dad.

"Nothing much. Just the usual. Classes, some catching up with friends and then ballet practice," I replied with a smile.

"Okay, okay, okay," dad replied back.

***

I understand by now that all of this is too confusing for you as I have really not shared anything about myself and just vented on about my life and my day. Let me explain it to you from the start and I guess everything will make sense to you.

My name's Isabella or as my parents and friends call me 'Belle'. I'm ten years old. I feel mature for my age but some people don't understand this (and by some, I mean most people). They still treat me like a baby – especially my relatives. I'm really fond of ballet and I've been practicing it for the past one year. I go for ballet classes which happen to be very close from my neighborhood. My parents say that it's always best to start early; either in sport, dance or music as the brain absorbs everything quickly and the body adapts to it extremely fast. Well, that's all fine and good but my toes really hurt. Anyways, we have this ballet recital coming which is due in less than three weeks and we are not even halfway through our performance.

I go to Oregan School which has grades right from 4th till 12th. It is a huge school and we've got people who barely manage to carry their books to people who shave right here in the locker room. I've got two best friends named Camille and Susan and right now, they aren't talking to me because I partnered up with someone else for my history project. Well, the truth is, I'm not good in history and my grades can't slip further. Rest all subjects are just fine.

For the project work, I partnered up with a boy called Liam and he will make sure that I do well in the project but these two don't seem to understand at all. Sometimes they could be real babies.

Anyways, I have an elder brother named Jason. He's a good big brother and has looked after me many times. For the past one year he has been acting a bit distant and has been quiet most of the time. I don't know what it is because whenever I would tell mom, she would just say, "It's just this age and you'll understand when you get there. Don't worry. I'm sure he still loves you."

Well, I just took her words as much. My mom's name is Emma (a pretty name) and my dad's name is Sam (eh – not so pretty). Anyways my mom and dad are always super busy. Both of them are called – um, what's the word that I'm looking for.. ah, yes, architects. They both are architects. And they have been designing some cool projects lately.

I have even visited a few of them. One is this beautiful park that is an hour away from our house, which has been designed by mom. As for my dad he has designed one of our neighboring schools. They both work in different companies and would always compete with each other, but in a healthy way, constantly upping each other's game by discussing their projects and helping each other out wherever required.

Mom and Dad are real foodies, and they are so energetic all the time. They constantly plan outings and dinner nights and we would also have occasional family game nights and what not. Apart from work, they have their own individual hobbies. Mom loves to paint, and dad writes novels in his free time. He has even published a few and I've read a couple of them. I really loved the ones that he has written recently, and he said that he has a few more in store for me. That's the reason I got into reading books.

I really don't know how they manage to do everything along with their busy work. Anyways I love my family. We constantly fly out to meet our grandparents as they stay in New Jersey and in Brooklyn.

Mom and dad both are the only child in their families so I don't really have any aunts or uncles but there are a few close friends of my mom and dad. Especially uncle Aaron. I love uncle Aaron; he brings the best presents and I guess I've known him for as long as I can remember. This is our cute family and I love it. Well, judging by this I'm sure that you might have understood that I love to chat…

***

Anyway, getting back to school: Jason and I arrived with five minutes to spare. At that time, the place was a complete circus—everyone was rushing to get to class. The elevators were always jammed, so taking the stairs was the best option. I reached my classroom while Jason went up to his; his was a floor above mine.

In history, we were given time for research over the weekend and even additional time during this period as well. Our history sir came, quietly sat down and began correcting papers. Liam and I began working but, I completely forgot to do my part over the weekend.

Our topic was on the French Revolution. Luckily Liam had prepared notes for both of us and that got me covered. I spent the time memorizing the lines for the presentation and before I got to the fourth page, the class got over.

After the class I wanted to go and sit with Susan and Camille, but they were still mad at me for not partnering with them. I was not too worried about it, and I was sure that this would last just a day or two more.

Then came the Spanish lecture. It was a rule that middle schools and high schools had to keep a second language as compulsory. There were a bunch of options given to us, but I decided to go for Spanish as it seemed the most interesting.

"Well class. Since we are done with the basic grammar rules, I am keeping a quiz of 15 points this coming week," said Ms. Aldrin, our Spanish teacher.

"Ugh," I said to myself.

I heard a small grunt next to me and I could see a collective sigh from everyone. Well great… I already had a dozen things to do over the weekend and this was added on top of it. I didn't have any choice in this one. I jotted down my to-do list as quickly as possible.

I spent the break with the rest of my classmates. We joined tables, put our lunchboxes on top, laughed alongside each other and ate our food. We girls spent most of the time talking and playing games on paper while the boys of our class did some mischief. They ran around the class and acted like a bunch of monkeys, just the same as usual.

After school Jason would go into his room and get lost in his own world. Our routine was the same, eat some snacks, relax and finish our homework. After a couple of hours, mom returned home and a little later, Dad came home too from work.

I rushed to my Mom and said, "I want to hang Taylor Swift's poster in my room, but Jason won't let me."

"Why, Jason, why are you giving trouble to your sister?"

"It's too girly, mother," Jason replied with a hint of frustration.

"Sure, but your 'Rolling Stones' logo with a funny tongue sticking out is no problem!" I screamed back at Jason.

Jason said nothing and went to his room, shut the door and started playing loud music.

"Ugh!! I hate you Jason," I said.

***

I had my ballet lessons at 7 and dad dropped me off at the studio. "I'm sorry I can't stay today, Belle. I must head back to the office. I'll be back on time to pick you up," he said.

The class was real fun, but things were starting to get hectic and Miss said that she would be keeping classes every day except on Sundays till the day of the performance.

Dad came and picked me up and we headed back home. As the weather at this time around was humid I wiped the sweat off my face and played some soft music on the radio.

"So how was your day today, Belle?" asked dad.

"Everything's going well daddy. It's just a bit tiring. Susan and Camille are still not talking to me. Plus, the ballet teacher said that she would be increasing classes to every day except Sundays till the play is not over."

"Ahh, I see!" replied my dad.

It was one of his signature looks – him pressing his lips firmly, his eyebrows trying to join each other, his nostrils flaring up a bit as he tried to see how he can make my situation a teensy bit easier.

"Well," he replied after a few seconds, "I'm not exactly sure if I can help you in ballet since you know I've never tried a ballet pose in my life but if you want, you can perform your routine for me and I can help you improve it and keep giving you suggestions. What say?"

"Thank you so much dad, you are the best," I said.

He smiled and said, "Well, as for the schoolwork, you've got to relax kiddo. I'm sure the test is a no biggie and don't worry about your friends. They'll come around. Alright??….."

I looked at him, giving him a weak smile as I turned my attention back to the radio. Dad was in a happy mood today. I could sense it.

"Let's see…… umm…. How do you feel about catching the new Chipmunk movie? We all can go out this weekend after your test. By then, most of my work would be completed. We can grab some Chinese food and have ice creams, chocolate chip flavor—the one you like. What say? Do we have a deal?"

"Hmm," I pretended to think but on the inside I was so happy. It sounded like a perfect day.

"Deal!" I exclaimed and shook his hand. He let out a soft laugh.

The next few days went more or less as planned. The history project which was due went fantastic for me. Liam helped me prep so well for it. Not only did he make my life easy, he made history easy for me. I got interested in the subject. Finally Mom and dad would be really proud of me.

After our first period Liam showed me his model for another presentation which was due tomorrow. Even though we didn't need a detailed model, his battlefield made of mud—with tiny soldiers and horses—was incredible. He beamed with pride as I helped with the finishing touches.

"Dude, the teacher will stand up and applaud tomorrow. I know it!'" Liam said with excitement.

"Hahaha, I am sure Liam. All the best and thank you for all your help," I said.

That's exactly what happened. While the teacher

didn't stand up, but he did applaud, and the class joined in as well. Some were happy, others a bit jealous, but I was overjoyed. Liam really had a knack for this.

In contrast, Camille and Susan had a rough day. They were unprepared, with their PowerPoint just a sloppy copy-paste job. The slides were a mess, and they couldn't answer any of the professor's questions. The class was silent, and the professor eventually told them to return to their seats with a hint of pity. Camille and Susan seemed even angrier at me, even though I had nothing to do with their lack of preparation. I just kept my distance for the rest of the day.

***

I came home. Jason and I were supposed to make sandwiches together for dinner. Mom and dad would be working till late today, I still wasn't allowed to switch on the gas when no one was at home. Jason was out somewhere as usual—god knows where. I tried calling him from the landline at our place but he didn't pick up. I tried again but there was no answer.

It was almost nine o' clock now. I was starting to get a bit worried. I called mom and told her everything. She sounded extremely mad on the phone and Jason was sure to get a scolding. I tried telling her to relax but she got even more worked up. I ate some cookies from my snacks. I practiced my ballet routine a couple of times and prepared for my Spanish test.

I heated my dinner in the microwave that was kept for me. Mom and dad came back at around nine thirty and mom was extremely furious.

"Where is your brother?" she asked in a stern voice.

I just shrugged my shoulders in a 'I don't know' manner. Jason finally showed up to the house at ten in the night and when he entered the room he was met by my angry parents.

"Where the hell have you been Jason?" shouted my mother.

I was told to go to my room, but I could still hear the voices from the living room. Mom and dad really let Jason have it. He got a pretty good scolding. When he finally entered my room, he seemed furious, and his face was all red. He looked at me in anger and shouted, "What was the need to call and tell mom that I haven't been home and just for once can't you make a simple sandwich on your own?" He was really upset and angry at the same time.

"I was just getting worried…," I replied. He wouldn't let me talk. I didn't understand where he had been. He just took his blanket and went outside. I tried to fall asleep.

I couldn't seem to stop making everyone upset.

***

The next day, I woke up early, eager for ballet practice after school. With no homework except for a simple Art assignment. I planned to finish my project so I could hang out with my building friends later. Jason, however, was unusually quiet—barely speaking to anyone, even our parents. I found out he'd been grounded for two weeks and missed his friend's birthday party, which only made him more agitated. Being around him felt like walking on thin ice.

After revising for my Spanish quiz, I headed to ballet practice. It was exhausting but rewarding; two-thirds of our routine was complete, and everyone was nailing their parts. After dinner, I met my friends for a stroll, but suddenly remembered I needed materials for my Art project. I quickly excused myself and rushed home.

I pulled out the list: watercolour set, 50 cm scale, 2B pencils, drafting pen, A4 sheets, and a Mount Board. I managed to find everything except the Mount Board. Panic set in—I didn't want to bother my parents, who were already stressed. Then it hit me: their study was filled with supplies. I'd seen it before, cluttered with art materials, papers, and boards.

I sneaked into the study, hoping to find what I needed. The room was even messier than I remembered—computers displaying floor plans, stacks of sheets, and crumpled papers everywhere. Amidst the chaos, I spotted a Mount Board and set it aside. The drafting pen was harder to find, but I finally located one in a drawer.

As I rummaged through the drawer, I stumbled upon a thick stack of papers with the title *Seven Lives Of Life.* It looked like a novel draft—something my dad had been working on. He was an incredible writer, with several published books, and I often helped him brainstorm ideas. But this title was new to me, and the manuscript looked old, like it had been forgotten.

Curiosity got the better of me. I grabbed the stack along with the Mount Board and pen, and quietly slipped back to my room. That night, I couldn't sleep, too intrigued by the manuscript. Once the house was silent, I turned on my reading light, and the bold title gleamed up at me: *Seven Lives Of Life.*

I flipped the first page and began to read.

CHAPTER 2

PROBLEMS

My head hurt so bad as I struggled to reach for my phone to shut off the damn alarm. As I did so, I barely managed to open my eyes and was blinded by the bright lights in my room. I dragged myself out of the bed, my head still spinning. I started looking around for my glasses. "Oh no! Did I sit on them again? God, I hope not," I whispered, silently praying.

I kept on searching for them, shuffling the bedsheets, and pulling the pillows out of the way. I was practically blind without them. The entire room was just a stretch of blurry shapes. All I could make out was just the basic outline of things and oh yes..I felt them and put them on immediately. Yup, a whole lot better. I dragged myself out of the bed. I had barely gotten two hours of sleep last night; too much Call of Duty—never again.

I know, I know. Every day I promised myself that I wouldn't play the damn game or maybe just one round, but I always ended up sweating it and before I knew it, there were only a couple of hours left for me to get up from my sleep.

I dragged my fat ass out of bed and trotted over to the bathroom. After splashing some cold water on my face to get rid of my sleep, I went over to the dressing table and looked at myself in the mirror. My stomach seemed even more bloated than usual. 'Shouldn't have eaten that last piece of pie'. The Chinese food alone was more than my usual meal, but this was just another one of my overeating stories. My cheeks were popping out, much more than usual. Even my nose—oh I hated my nose, this squashed piece of fruit on my face. I was ridiculed for it almost every single day; atleast one nasty comment about it everyday. Ok, I had to get going. Enough of staring at myself for today.

So ya, the usual routine. Another crappy day to get on with. I just remembered about the homework that was due today. Great! Another detention to look forward to. The day hadn't even properly begun, and things were already starting to get on my nerves. I changed into some school clothes, sprayed some perfume, grabbed a cup of coffee, and ran out of the house with my school bag dangling from my left arm.

Tenth grade was just too much for me to handle. I barely managed to scrape through school all these years and I was honestly at a breaking point. Why does life have to be so miserable? What was even the point of going to school? Where was I going to apply the laws of trigonometry in my life? And, why should I learn about my country's history and let alone my country?

If that wasn't enough, I had to deal with English Literature. Oh, my lord! These English authors from the past—I hated them more than anyone else. They couldn't just let things be. Why couldn't they accept that curtains were blue because they were blue, and leave it at that? Instead, they had to find meaning in every color and relate it to moods and thoughts. Why complicate things so much? I don't even remember the color of my own curtains. The whole schooling system felt like a scam—waste of time and money. Teachers were fed up with me, hardly anyone talked to me in class, and I lost my phone privileges almost every weekend. All I have is my stupid hamster, Mort. We have one thing in common: both of us sit around all day, wondering why our lives are so pointless. Mort just lazes around, sometimes flat on his back or slumped in a corner, making me even more bored and lazy.

Most of my classmates were jerks. During the entirety of school, they kept pulling juvenile pranks on me. Even though I requested them for the 100th time to stop it, they simply wouldn't listen. Even when I complained to the teacher that didn't help me at all, instead she would just act oblivious towards everything. This just made me a bigger target instead.

If I were a teacher's pet, things might have been different. For example, last Friday, during the lecture before break, someone had placed a bucket of dirty water on top of the classroom door, leaving it slightly ajar. As I returned from art class and opened the door, the bucket came crashing down on me. The entire class roared with laughter. It might have seemed funny to them, but it wasn't at all amusing when I was drenched in foul-smelling water, which took a week of shampooing and scrubbing twice a day to get rid of.

I was so flustered that I immediately ran out of the classroom. I often got blamed for things I had no part in. For instance, two guys were monkeying around, wrestling, and jumping on each other. One of them ended up carrying the other on his shoulders. With the extra weight, he lost his balance, and they both crashed onto a desk, flipping it over with a loud bang. Thankfully, they were alright, but the desk had a big crack.

The next day, the homeroom teacher saw the damage and demanded, "Who did this?" One of the boys shouted, "Ma'am, it was Trevor's doing," and another added, "Yes, I saw it too!" Everyone nodded in agreement. I ended up with three days of detention, two hours each, because the teacher preferred to assign blame rather than listen to the whole story.

I felt like punching those guys, but I knew they would just gang up on me. I never really connected with any of my classmates. My stammering didn't help when it came to making friends. Whenever I tried to introduce myself or make conversation, I'd end up stammering, "Hii I... II, thiss is Tr..ee.vvor. Iii just just waaannteddd wanted to knowwwwww...," and people would either move away or make fun of me. There was no point in trying to talk to them. School felt hopeless. Most days, I'd fixate on the clock, wishing for time to pass quickly so I could get home.

The only exception was Rose. She was one of the smartest and prettiest girls in my class. Everything about her was pleasing to the eye. She excelled at almost everything and was in the school volleyball team. I, on the other hand, felt like a volleyball with arms and legs. I always wanted to tell her how I felt, not expecting much in return, but I was too scared to admit it. The thought of doing so made me feel like I would die of embarrassment.

She was always good to me. I was paired with her a couple of times, for either some assignment or another group project and she was always very sweet to me. But I always got the feeling, that she was stuck with me. Apart from her, no one even looked at me, all of them would just see through me. Today's day was pretty much like any other school day. I barely managed to survive the first three lectures just to be bombarded with a double math lecture after recess. I tried to complete my homework during the break, but I couldn't make head or tail out of the problems. I just prayed that the teacher would forget about it.

The class proceeded as usual, with one lecture almost over. The teacher rambled on about algebra concepts, and I was relieved she had forgotten to ask about the homework. But my relief was short-lived. A little nerd piped up, "Ma'am, don't forget about the homework!"

"Oh, yes! Thank you, Violet," she said cheerfully. I could see her grin as she remembered. Just what I needed.

One by one, she called each student to her desk and checked their homework meticulously. When it was my turn, I approached the desk, clutching my book. I whispered, "I didn't complete the assigned work."

"Well, Trevor! Just as I expected from you," she said, her smile fading. She stood up and made me face the class. "Repeat that so everyone can hear," she demanded.

I mumbled, "I didn't do the homework."

She screamed at me for ten minutes straight. "I have never seen such a pathetic student in my entire teaching career. How do you continue to be such a troublesome child? Sometimes I feel it's my fault that I couldn't make anything out of you. I guarantee you this, Trevor: if you keep up this rate, you'll be stuck in the tenth grade for at least another two years!"

I had taken a lot of shouting in my life but never had I been insulted so badly in front of the entire class. It really struck a nerve. Not only did she scream at me for ten minutes straight, but she humiliated me and made me stand at my desk for the rest of the lecture. After this torture, only English was left.

I doodled in my notebook as the English teacher rambled on about some Shakespeare play, The Merchant of Venice. My mind wandered to dinner, and once again, I found myself hating every bit of school. It was worth repeating: I HATE SCHOOL. I came home, looking as glum as ever and already a couple of hours late than usual. I glanced at my watch and realized I'd have to come up with another excuse, though I had exhausted every possibility. I rang the doorbell and, like a sad sack, trudged inside.

Mom called from the kitchen, "Detention again? What did you do this time?"

I could tell her the truth, but I wasn't in the mood for another lecture about completing work on time and how the teachers were doing it for my own good. I simply replied, "It wasn't my fault," and went to my room. After a quick lunch and a few episodes of The Office, I opened my homework book and stared blankly at the English assignment: a book report on The Merchant of Venice.

"Well, this is going to be a disaster," I muttered to myself. I hadn't read the play, wasn't even sure if I had the title right. I stared at my blank notebook, trying to recall something—anything—to write. When nothing came to mind, I gave up and typed "Merchant of Venice Cliff Notes" into my laptop. In seconds, the summary appeared on my screen. "Perfect," I said, feeling a bit of relief.

I copied everything down line by line and finished the

assignment in about fifteen minutes. I should have shuffled the content to avoid detection, but I was too lazy. I shut the book, tossed it near my bag, and left the room. Bored and annoyed, I noticed it was already six in the evening due to the stupid detention.

Mom had prepared some food, so I grabbed a plate and took it to my room. As I settled in to play one of my shows, Dad came home late. I heard the rattling of keys and the door opening. "Oh no," I groaned. I quickly shut off the PS4, tossed the controller aside, folded my glasses, and lay down, pulling the blanket over my head.

Dad's footsteps approached my room. "Is Trevor in there?" he asked.

Mom replied from the kitchen, "He should be. I heard him come in a while ago."

Dad's footsteps grew closer, and I held my breath. The door to his room opened, and I heard him go inside and close it. I let out a sigh of relief. If he knew I was still up playing video games, he would be furious. I thought about playing games on mute but decided against it. I closed my eyes and tried to sleep.

Before I knew it, the alarm rang again. Oh God! This was one of the worst possible dreams—and a weird one at that. I had been resting peacefully when suddenly, I found myself locked in the basement of a ship, tied up by pirates. The place was dark as a dungeon, and I was surrounded by others in the same predicament. The ship rocked, and I could feel the movement.

Huge wooden barrels stood around, and dirty old ropes and crumpled scrolls were scattered about. The door suddenly burst open, and a harsh light flooded the room. As my eyes adjusted, I saw a tall, nasty-looking pirate laughing loudly. To my horror, I recognized him as my science professor.

"Professor?" I gasped. "What is this?"

He cut the ropes binding me and removed the cloth from my mouth. "Ouch!" I winced as my jaw ached. "What's going on?" I asked, but before I could get an answer, he hurled me out the door into the sunlight.

I looked around: it was a massive ship surrounded by deep blue water with no land in sight. On deck were more pirates, many of whom looked familiar. It was a mix of my classmates and school teachers, all in pirate costumes.

Christian, a classmate I loathed, stood at the steering wheel, laughing just like the pirate professor. "Look who it is, it's T-T-Trevor," he mocked, imitating my stutter.

"Christian! What the hell?" I shouted, fuming. "Why are you doing this?"

Christian sneered, "Just having some fun. This is your nightmare, not ours!"

The math teacher appeared, grinning with a few broken teeth. "Ah, Trevor," he said, his voice dripping with malice. "You're just in time for your final test."

"What? No!" I cried. "What's happening?"

The pirate professor approached slowly, a knife in hand. "He's not going to kill me, is he?" I thought, trembling.

He picked me up by the collar and whispered menacingly, "You know what you have to do, don't you?"

"No…no… I-I really don't," I stammered, terrified. His chilling black eyes and unkempt appearance only added to my fear.

"Oh, you don't know what you're supposed to do?" he asked with a sinister smile. "Let me tell you then."

He turned to the crew and shouted, "Walk the plank… ARRRGHHHH!"

The pirates roared with excitement, and I was pushed towards the plank. My classmates and teachers surrounded me, brandishing shiny swords and poking me with them. "Ouch, this isn't funny… it really hurts!" I protested, but they ignored me, treating my fear as entertainment.

"Move it, Trevor!" Christian yelled, pushing me forward.

I stepped onto the plank, the ship rocking beneath me. Below was nothing but the vast ocean. I was shivering and struggling to keep my balance as the pirates continued to prod me. With no other option, I took a deep breath, stood on my tiptoes, and suddenly lost my balance, falling into the depths below.

I screamed as I plummeted, and then I woke up, sitting straight in bed. I fumbled for my glasses and put them on, drenched in sweat. What a horrible dream! I looked in the mirror, checked that I was alright, and tried to get back to sleep. It took half an hour, but I finally managed to drift off. Then, the alarm blared again. I groaned into my pillow, knowing I had to get up. A few more minutes of procrastination, and Mom would be in my room, furious. The last thing I needed to start my day.

CHAPTER 3

EMBARRASSMENT

I rushed to the bathroom. I had exactly twenty minutes before I had to get out of the house and be at the school. I removed my uniform and freshened up in the bathroom. I was making good time when suddenly, I had to rush back again to the bathroom. A big poop was coming; I could feel it. I immediately rushed back into the bathroom and sat down. My stomach felt wobbly and was even hurting for a bit. I just sat like that, holding my stomach and after after I was finally done, I looked at my watch. "Oh shit!! I was already so late.

School would begin in literally five minutes. I pulled up my pants, squeezed into them and just rushed out of there. I grabbed my bag from the hall and was out the door in a second. I could hear my mom shouting from the dining table.

"At least have a slice."

"Later!" I screamed as I shut the door behind me.

Oh no, I was going to be so late. I immediately rushed out of there. I looked around, thankfully there was a cab right around. I sat in it and immediately told the driver, "Woodwark Avenue.... Go go go!"

Oh no. I would have to climb the stairs again. The last

couple of times, I could barely make it to the top. I almost passed out. Even just climbing one floor was a tough task for me. First, my legs had to lift myself up, and then on top of that, I had to carry this heavy bag. Oh God! I reached the base of the staircase in maybe what was like twenty minutes. My school was very strict when it came to things regarding discipline, such as punctuality, attendance, and all that stuff. I reached the place, and no, I wasn't allowed to take the lift.

"Please, just this once? My legs are killing me," I pleaded with the guard, who didn't even bother to look up from his newspaper.

"No exceptions," he grunted, flipping the page.

I sighed, knowing arguing would get me nowhere. Ten more minutes late, and I wouldn't be allowed to even enter the building. I looked at the staircase, and so it began—the journey of twelve floors, each one bringing more pain than the previous.

"Well, here we go," I muttered to myself, gripping the railing and taking that first dreaded step.

The first floor was already a struggle. My ankle and feet started throbbing with pain. My bag felt like it weighed a ton. It was as if I was carrying boulders instead of books. I paused to catch my breath.

"Keep moving!" a teacher yelled from above as she walked past me.

"Easy for you to say," I mumbled under my breath, dragging myself up another step.

By the time I reached the fourth floor, my tight-fitting pants, which were already on the verge of ripping, finally gave up and let out a loud rip.

"Seriously?" I groaned, glancing around to see if anyone noticed. Luckily, the stairwell was empty. But it just had to be over there—the most embarrassing spot possible.

I pushed on, determined to reach the top, but by the time I hit the eighth floor, my stomach began to cramp up. The pain was unbearable. I couldn't take another step. I collapsed on the cold floor, lying flat near the staircase.

A passing teacher spotted me and sighed heavily. "You again? Why am I not surprised?" she said, shaking her head.

"Help… please…" I croaked out, too exhausted to even sit up.

"Go get someone," she instructed an eighth-grader who had been standing nearby, staring at me with wide eyes. The kid nodded and ran off, returning a few minutes later with another teacher. Together, they hauled me to my feet.

"Come on, let's get you to class," the teacher said, clearly annoyed. The eighth-grader was struggling to hold up my bag, looking like he regretted getting involved.

"I'm so sorry," I muttered as they practically dragged me up the last few flights of stairs.

By the time we reached my classroom, I was thirty minutes late, and the first lecture was almost over. The teacher gave me a withering look as I stumbled inside.

"Nice of you to join us, Mr.," she said sarcastically, causing the entire class to erupt in laughter.

I slunk into my seat, my face burning with embarrassment.

"Hey look," shouted Christian, the fatty has torn his pants from behind."

"Everyone look, look" and all eyes were at me. I awkwardly stuffed myself between the desk and the chair while the entire

class was howling, shouting, and having a blast. I couldn't have been more embarrassed. I just stared at the desk, looking down and then I heard a soft sound.

"Hey" I turned around and looked. It was Rose and she was holding a black jacket in her hand. "Wrap this around your waist," she said.

"Don't worry about the others," I replied softly and said thank you.

I wrapped the jacket around my waist and just sat quietly till the end of the lecture.

For another ten minutes the teacher discussed the Cold War with the class and I tuned everything out, feeling humiliated and bullied.

Aww… this was too awful. I felt a little bad laughing along as I read about his pants getting torn but this really was very sad. I couldn't help but feel pity for this poor kid. At least this girl was the one helpful to this poor boy.

This seemed one hell of a story. Judging by the style of writing, I was certain that this was my dad's doing. How could he have kept this from me? I was his biggest supporter. I flipped the pages till the end to see and yup! It seemed like a complete, solid script. I just pondered about everything that I had just read and couldn't believe what was going on. The story certainly seemed interesting, and I couldn't wait to see what was next! I looked at my brother, looking so peaceful in his deep sleep. Wish he would've been the same when he was awake.

CHAPTER 4

ALONE

My eyes seemed extremely droopy, yet a part of me didn't want to stop reading. I had forgotten to finish up a couple of things—which would probably help me stay awake for a bit longer. I gathered my notebooks, pouch, sheets and packed my school bag. I gave a final touch-up to my 'almost-complete' assignment and decided on my outfit for tomorrow. And last but not least, I snuck into the kitchen, and made myself a glass of hot cocoa to pair well with this novel and continued reading.

Next came the English lecture. I couldn't take it anymore, I just wanted to go home.

"Today would really be a good day for a smoke," I thought to myself.

I remember the first time I tried weed. It was about a year ago. I was on my way home from school, feeling extremely low and dejected. As I passed by a restaurant, I noticed a half-lit joint resting on the windowsill. I glanced around to make sure no one was watching. Slowly, I reached out and picked it up. It was a small, rolled piece of paper, something I had only ever seen in movies and stories. I hesitated for a moment, then brought it to my lips and took a small drag. Almost instantly, a harsh cough erupted from my throat, and I quickly put it down, feeling unsure of what I'd just experienced.

I just went on home not thinking much about it and just washed my mouth with a cola. Soon I learnt about this one person—a young guy who had a coffee cart stall next to the restaurant and was known dealing in this stuff. I decided I wanted to try the joint properly, but this time in my home and taking my own sweet time. I knew that it was a big risk, but I couldn't do all of this in a hurry and out in the open. But the coffee guy was stubborn. He wasn't keen on selling to a fourteen-year-old, which, in hindsight, was probably reasonable. Finally, after agreeing to pay almost double the usual price, he relented and gave me some. It took a big chunk out of my savings.

I had kept that stash hidden in my sock drawer for a long long time. I remember the first time I tried it peacefully at home. It relaxed me a lot and I felt extremely carefree. I rarely smoked it but the times that I did, it was really something else.

Woah what!! I exclaimed in and let out a little squeal. And then I realized what was he talking about. This boy's shenanigans just never seemed to end. I looked around to ensure that I didn't wake anyone. I turned to see Jason, but he was out cold, snuggling with the blanket as a trail of drool was formed on his pillow. Ew!

Intrigued or call it curious, I continued reading the book. Although it was way past my bedtime.

Next came the history professor. I took out my books and tried my level best to remain focused during the lecture but after a while, I started to drift off. I hardly got any sleep last night and I couldn't stop myself from dozing off. You'd think after having such a 'delightful' morning and being screamed at loudly, I would be wide awake. A normal student might be but this wasn't something totally out of the blue for me. I had taken up such crap from everyone. I couldn't really call anyone as my friend. I was the kind of person that everyone just took for granted. This was the case for every year and most of my batches. I had no real friends from this batch because it was the worst, but even the previous ones weren't too great.

Aww.. I couldn't help but feel sad for the poor fella. I could see him sitting all alone and just minding his business.

Even among the few students who spoke to me, most eventually moved away just because the others didn't want to be seen with me. The one guy who was genuinely my closest friend was Alex, but even he left me. Well, that's a story for another day. I continued staring at the whiteboard as Ms. Miranda droned on. Finally, I glanced at my watch—just ten minutes left in the lecture. I couldn't wait any longer and excused myself to go to the bathroom.

"Haven't you made a big enough hole in your pants already?" someone yelled from the back of the class, and the room erupted in laughter.

"Silence!" Miss Miranda shouted.

I ignored the comment, left the room, and checked the mirror in the bathroom. Sure enough, there was a noticeable tear in the back of my pants, my underwear clearly visible. Great. I was stuck like this for the rest of the day.

I killed some more time in the bathroom, wandering the hallways until the class was over. I spotted my history teacher exiting the classroom and debated going back in. But honestly, what was the point? More ridicule, more taunts. I could just picture them grabbing my jacket and running off with it. I wasn't in the mood to chase anyone around the building.

So, I decided to take a stroll, aimlessly wandering the halls. I had about ten or fifteen minutes to kill. As I loitered near the fifth-floor washroom, the school bell rang loudly. I had no idea what class was next, but I certainly didn't want to be late again. I rushed back to my classroom, slid into my seat, and then it hit me—the English teacher was already there, and I hadn't finished the book report. Ah, great. Just my luck today.

Mrs. Roberts, our English teacher, entered the room in a huff. She was usually cheerful, one of the few bearable teachers, but today she looked anything but happy. She dropped her stuff onto the desk, her spectacles perched at the edge of her nose as she scanned the room, her mind clearly elsewhere. After a minute of silence, she opened her laptop and began typing furiously. The entire class sat in silence, not daring to speak.

Suddenly, she looked up from her screen, her eyes narrowing. "What are you all staring at? Didn't I give you assignments to complete? Take them out now, and I want everyone to present them loudly to the class."

She paused, then pointed straight at me. "You go first."

I awkwardly looked at her and got up from my seat with the notebook in my hand. I was very hesitant to read out my work, but I immediately began to read as I didn't want to test her patience. I started reading out my work, "Antonio, a leading merchant of Venice, is a wealthy, respected, and popular man. Among his many friends is a young man named Bassanio, who owes Antonio a good deal of money. Bassanio would like to repay his friend….."

I looked at her but she gave no indication or no reaction at all. So I continued reading and was halfway through, 'At this point, Portia, disguised as a lawyer, and Nerissa, dressed as her law clerk, enter the court and 'tell the Duke that they have been sent from Padua by a learned attorney.'

Mrs. Roberts completed my statement with the exact same words and looked up from her laptop.

"Tell me Trevor, do you think I am a fool?" she asked me in a calm yet daunting voice.

"No, miss," I replied in fear.

"I beg your pardon! You think that I'm a fool sitting here and assigning all of you work so that you can copy paste it from the internet." By this point she had started shouting. "I have been teaching for the past 15 years. I've seen students copy word to word from the cliff notes that are present on the net. Some modify it slightly, but you have not even bothered to do that much. What am I going to do with you... do you have any interest in studying at all? You just simply come here to show your face. Wasting your mom and dad's money."

I had no idea what to say. I just stood there, staring at her. Of course, everything had to go wrong today. Mrs. Roberts looked furious.

"I need a completely new book report done by tomorrow," she snapped. "And you're going to write the entire thing three times. If it's not done, you'll have me to answer to!"

I nodded, defeated, and slunk back to my seat. She moved on to the next student, and one by one, everyone presented their work. I sat there, trying to blend into my chair, completely fed up with everything.

The rest of the day dragged on, just like always—same routine, same monotony. But that dream I had last night kept replaying in my mind, over and over again.

***

"Oh man this kid was in a big, big trouble," I thought to myself. The start sounded like fun. I looked at the watch and oh my god! It was already half past eleven. I better go to sleep, but I really wanted to go on reading. I couldn't possibly stay up any longer and even if I did, I really wouldn't be able to get up and go to school tomorrow.

The next day at school I was really bored. The same usual drama went on and I was just excited to get back home and continue with the story. The art teacher instructed us to start our work. I had brought the required materials—everything was ready.

Luckily there wasn't much homework for today. So, I just completed the rest of the work and quietly put the new mount board and the old drafting back in their original places. Later I went to my recital. After I was done with today's jobs I hopped onto bed with my comfortable nightdress and continued with the story. I slowly turned the pages.

I took the train to come back home. I just wanted to roam a bit and not get back home immediately. I wasted an hour loitering here and there. I stopped at a couple of shops. I was thinking of trying to kill some time when I saw a Supermarket at the opposite side. It looked like a brand new one, with the words 'Supermarket' highlighted in bright red letters, printed onto the board. I entered the place. The entire thing was massive. It's ends stretched all the way to the other side. I spent at least an hour roaming around, exploring each aisle. I looked at the huge frozen yogurt section, the cold cuts section. All of it was so tempting, it felt heavenly.

The entire section was titled, 'The Sweet Spot'. In it there were at least a hundred different types of candies, chocolates, sugar mints, fruit rollups, sweets from all over the world—basically anything sweet that was ever invented was present over there. That too in different shapes and sizes—round, rolled up, square, hexagon and what not, and in every possible colour.

My mouth started watering just by looking at all of this. I wish I could stay here forever. I took out my wallet just to see if I could get something right now. I had a couple of singles and some change. I grabbed a box of grape flavoured icebreakers and went to get it billed. I stepped out of the place reluctantly and headed back home.

My god! This boy really liked to eat. I could picture a fat kid with plump cheeks stuffing himself with loads of candies. It certainly painted a funny picture and was kinda cute.

I would try to talk to my parents about my problems, but their advice was always the same: keep making efforts to improve yourself. They believed that distancing myself from others to avoid bad experiences was pointless. But it wasn't that I hadn't tried before. Maybe kids today are just different. No one really cares about you unless you're good at something. That's the part my parents didn't understand. Even after talking to them, I knew I was on my own. They were there for 'emotional support,' but in reality, it all came down to me.

When I finally got home, I rang the bell, but no one answered. I tried again—still nothing. Annoyed, I pulled out my keys and let myself in. The house was eerily quiet as I headed straight to my room. After freshening up, I caught a glimpse of myself in the mirror. "God, could my cheeks spread out any more?" I muttered.

Stepping out of the bathroom, I fired up the PlayStation and threw myself onto the bed, but not before shedding that stupid uniform. I tossed Rose's black jacket onto the side table, ready to escape into my virtual world for a while.

I looked around and saw Mort nicely lying in his playpen. I would even sometimes talk about my issues to Mort, and I would pretend that he could understand them but all he ever did was roll around in his own dirt. It was just nice knowing that there was someone to tell how I was feeling.

I looked at him. I used to leave him out all the time but then he would create havoc like anything. He would run around the house, and would crawl through such tiny spaces. It was impossible to keep a track of him. Dad wasn't too fond of him and by this point, nor was I. He was too much work. I had to give him food from time to time, and even if I let the cage open, I had to always keep a track of wherever he went, to make sure he wasn't putting himself in danger. Sometimes I would even forget to feed him, and then mom would look at me and give me the lecture of responsibility and blah, blah blah…

I hardly ever took him out of the cage anymore. His once-brown fur had taken on a grayish tinge from the grime building up in his cage. And the cage? Don't even get me started. Cleaning it was just too much hassle. Bathing him and giving him a good scrub was out of the question. I barely took care of myself, so looking after him was a whole different story. It had been weeks since he'd had a proper bath. Now he just sat there, his belly hanging out as he sighed. His expression never changed, probably thinking, "What a lousy owner I have. I wish someone else would take care of me." Well, too bad for him. Life is full of disappointments.

I tossed my shirt into the wash and threw the pants into the bin. Feeling hungry, I went to check the kitchen and found a note on the refrigerator: "Gone grocery shopping, back by 8." I had almost three hours to myself. Instead of firing up my PS4, I decided to tackle the book report, not to be a "good boy," but because I had a better plan. I pulled out my laptop, researched everything about the book, edited my findings, watched videos, and summarized the key points. I was done in an hour, and not just once, but three times—just as the teacher had asked. I was a bit surprised and impressed with myself.

With the report out of the way, it was time for some fun. Dad wouldn't be back until around 8:30 or 9, and Mom was out until 8. I had two whole hours to myself. I went to my room, shut the curtains, and locked the door. I retrieved my stash from the sock drawer—a small packet that made my troubles disappear, at least temporarily.

"This is our little secret," I told Mort, who was too busy making dirt balls in his cage. I set up on my study table, lit the joint, and took a puff. Instantly, I felt better. I took another puff and let my mind wander. No one wanted to be friends with me. My parents didn't seem to care either. They were

there for "emotional support," but it felt like I was a burden. My classmates? They'd probably forget my name by the end of the semester. I took another puff and sank into relaxation.

Soon, I was so drowsy that I didn't notice when I fell asleep. A loud banging on the door jolted me awake. I glanced at the clock—it was already 8:30. I'd been asleep for almost two hours. "One minute, I'm opening the door!" I shouted. Panicking, I quickly stuffed the lighter, the used joint, and everything else into a plastic bag and shoved it into the sock drawer. I sprayed perfume around the room, splashed water on my face, and straightened myself before opening the door.

Mom looked at me, puzzled. "Why was the door locked for so long?"

"Nothing," I replied. "I was just really tired. School has been hectic, and I needed a nap. I didn't want to be disturbed, so I locked the door. I woke up because of your knocking. Thanks for that!"

She gave me a sarcastic look but didn't press further. I closed the door and collapsed onto the bed. That was a close call. A whiff of that smoke, and I would have been in serious trouble. My head was still spinning, so I decided to go back to sleep and deal with tomorrow. I called out, "No dinner for me. I'm too tired and full. I'll see you at breakfast." I was too lazy to walk to the kitchen. I heard a soft "Alright" from Mom and shut the door.

The next morning, I arrived at school early—probably the earliest I'd ever been. I certainly didn't want a repeat of yesterday. I walked in and saw a few students already there. As the class filled up, everyone ignored me except for one person who stopped only to crack a joke about my stutter or my figure. I shrugged it off. The noise and chatter of the class were relentless, and I thought, "Couldn't these people ever be quiet for once?"

First class was English. I handed my book report to the teacher, who looked over it and nodded. "I'll review this in detail," she said. I replied, "Sure, ma'am," and went back to my seat. After class, I returned the jacket to Rose.

I managed to avoid scolding for the rest of the day and kept to myself. Thankfully, I had slept well. At lunch, my tiffin contained rice and pulses—food I couldn't stand. I went to McDonald's for a Big Mac, large fries, and a chocolate smoothie. The meal was a delight, a welcome break from home-cooked food that Mom rarely let me enjoy. Fast-food joints were my second home, especially McDonald's, which stayed open until 2 a.m. I often snuck out for late-night cravings, and the staff even knew me well enough to let me take leftover food.

After savoring my meal, I paid and tossed my tiffin's contents into the nearest trash can. I headed home, stuffed and satisfied, and made it back in about 7-10 minutes, already sweating from the brisk pace.

Okay now this kid didn't sound cute. He just sounded spoilt and ungrateful for God's sake. I mean disrespecting the food prepared by his mom, tossing it like that seemed so bad. He was just a spoiled brat.

I closed the book and put my yellow-coloured sunflower bookmark between the pages and kept it in my bottommost drawer. I shut the lights and drifted off to sleep.

CHAPTER 5

BAD DECISIONS

The artwork in school was exciting than I had thought. We had to first create a beautiful sketch of our favourite landscape on the Mount Board and then darken the outline with charcoaled pencils. We had to cover the paper to protect the lines and then add a splash of water colours to the entire thing. It was a beautiful illustration of a pretty landscape standing out in a myriad of colours.

The tall cliff overlooking the beautiful animal kingdom with thousands of animals that were looking like ants stretched across the vast green surface of the forest. I carefully placed the project in the locker. Most of us decided to leave our projects in the school itself since it was too much work to bring it back and forth for the next coming days.

I could feel my classmates rolling their eyes as the teacher praised my painting. But honestly, it did look pretty good. After school, I went home, finished some work, and then headed to my recital. Once the lights dimmed, I picked up the stapled set of sheets, pulled out my bookmark, and continued reading.

I took out my keys and as soon as I opened the door, I came face to face with an angry woman—my mother—who was angrier than I had ever seen her. She would get upset quite often but this was something else. Her entire face was red, the vein on her forehead almost ready to pop and there were tears in her eyes. In one hand, she held a Stats test paper that I had kept hidden—in which I apparently hadn't done too well. I had completely forgotten about it. I tried to reason with her about my tremendous marks, but that surprise was nothing compared to the one she had in the other hand as she pulled out a bag—not just an ordinary one—in it was my stash of weed.

"Oh shitt!" I thought. I knew I was done for.

She threw the bag onto the floor and screamed in anger and despair. "What the hell Trevor. Drugs! What's wrong with you. Have you totally lost it? Your room was so messed up that I had to assemble it. In what kind of pity state do you live in?

Why were you going through my stuff? Why did you open my cupboard when I wasn't there?" I shot back, but quickly fell silent. I had no defense.

"What did you just say?" she asked, her voice rising. "What the hell is the matter with you, Trevor? You're getting worse day by day, and just when I thought you couldn't sink any lower, you prove me wrong!"

She took a pause, controlled her anger and then continued, "I was keeping some of your clothes back into your cupboard and that is when I saw the used-up joint placed nicely at the side, next to your towels. To my surprise when I searched your cupboard I found this bag of weed stuffed in your sock drawer. Since how long have you been doing this?" she asked.

I knew I had screwed up—big time. I tried everything to

avoid her gaze but this angered her even more.

"Look at me when I'm talking to you. How long have you been into all of this? Do you even know what the hell you are taking. You're barely 16 years old. Do you have any idea of what is happening to your body?"

I stood there like a dumb person.

" What the hell is the matter with you. Enough is enough. I am done with all of this. I can't handle any more of all this. I have tried my level best to cope with you, but weed? It's time you are put back in your place."

Ohh no… what was this boy doing. Drugs! Really? When he was in high school or something like that. I didn't feel sorry for this boy at all anymore.

I knew this was it. I tried to get out of it by making excuses. "It belongs to a friend!" I pleaded. "I didn't even know where it came from!" But she wasn't having any of it. Her fury was unmistakable, and I knew my explanations were pathetic.

"Do you think I'm stupid?" she snapped, her voice trembling with anger. "You really expect me to believe that?"

Before I could respond, she slapped me hard across the right cheek. It was the first time my mom had ever raised her hand to me, and it hurt like hell. I could see the rage blazing in her eyes, and for the first time, I genuinely feared for my life. No amount of begging or pleading would get me out of this.

"Mom, please," I stammered, "I swear, it's not what you think."

But she cut me off, her voice cold and final. "Enough, Trevor. I don't want to hear another word."

I stood there, frozen, as she glared at me, her anger burning through the silence. Finally, she spoke, her tone icy.

"Wait till your dad gets home."

A chill ran down my spine. "Mom, no, please…"

"Go to your room, Trevor. Now."

Yup, mark the date. Today was the day I was officially going to die. I didn't say anything else. I didn't know what to say. I just turned and went to my room, the weight of what was coming crushing down on me.

I went into my room and just crashed onto the bed. I drifted off to sleep and was awakened by my angry mother.

I looked at the watch and figured Dad was probably home. I took a deep breath and stepped into the hall. He was sitting calmly at the table. He looked at the test paper, then at the bag of weed and finally, at me. His eyes stared straight into my soul. His eyes frozen, his hands shaking in anger as he looked at me. From over there itself, he totally lost it. He screamed at the top of his lungs and berated the shit out of me. Basically, it was a repeat of the fiasco with Mom, but with double the screaming and intensity.

All of this was too much to handle. I tried explaining everything, tried reasoning. I couldn't do much because I was pretty much guilty. All I could do was say sorry and I tried my level best to reason but, nothing could be done. After he was done yelling at me, he just simply said, "Go back to your room." Even in the past, whenever he spoke in that calm yet angry tone, there was no reasoning with him. I was sent back to my room, and I quietly obeyed.

I sat down on the bed, tossing and turning all night but unable to get a wink of sleep. I kept wondering what was going to happen to me. Knowing my parents, I was certain they weren't going to let me off the hook.

The next day I went down for breakfast. The hall was filled with stone cold silence. Dad had already left for work. Mom wasn't too interested in small talk. I asked about yesterday's incident and what was to be done; hoping and praying that they would just let it go. However, to my disappointment that wasn't the case.

"Mom, I am really sorry for everything. Can you please forget about everything," I said.

Mom mumbled, "We'll talk to you when you get back home."

Great! Another lecture to attend. As if the lectures in school weren't frying my brain.

But there was no point in arguing. I replied 'ok'; ate half a sandwich tossed the remaining half in the bin and left to get changed. Before leaving the room, I took a hard glance at my hamster—Mort. Just seeming him lazing around bothered me, more like irritated me.

Why did I have to do so much work and all he had to do was eat, poop and sleep? In a fit of anger, I lifted his cage and rattled his cage with such force—giving him the shock of his life. He jumped about in his cage and woke up startled. I let out an evil laugh and tossed the cage onto the floor. Slamming the door behind me, I headed downstairs.

"What?! That's so cruel and rude," I thought, feeling a pang of empathy for the poor hamster. I understood his anger, but hurting an innocent creature? With an exaggerated sigh, I continued reading.

I arrived at the school, and it was the same story all over again. Yelling of students, homework, me being shouted at by teachers, other students gossiping.

I came back home and freshened up. I sat on my bed and fired up the PlayStation. I started playing and got so wrapped up in it that I didn't even realize how quickly time flew by. Before I knew it, it was already evening—time for my judgment to be passed.

Suddenly, Mom opened the door, startling me for a second. She already wasn't in a great mood, and seeing the controller in my hand only made her more flustered.

"Get downstairs," she snapped. "Your dad and I need to talk to you."

I knew this was serious. When I got to the living room, Dad was waiting, his expression grim. They both sat me down, and Mom started in with the usual lecture.

"Trevor, we're really disappointed in the way you're leading your life," she began. "Your attitude toward everything is so cynical. You never take interest in your studies or anything around the house."

Dad chimed in, his voice stern. "We've given you everything you've ever wanted, and this is how you repay us? By being spoiled and careless?"

I kept my head low, patiently waiting for the inevitable punishment. I knew better than to argue back. "We've waited long enough for you to get your life back on track," Mom continued, her tone hardening. "But now, we're going to handle it our way."

Uh-oh, I thought to myself, feeling a knot tighten in my stomach.

"If you're ever caught with a cigarette or weed again," Dad said, his voice dropping ominously, "you're going straight to rehab—whether you think you have a problem or not.

And if you fail your boards, you'll be sent straight to boarding school. No more chances, Trevor."

This was the last straw! I knew I was done for. The only way out of this was for me to open my books and start studying. I decided that I needed to get my act together. I created my study timetable and decided to throw away even my secret stash but ended up keeping it—big mistake. There were only ten days left for my exams and all I had to do was pass my test.

I studied a bit each day but was still unsure whether I would be able to clear these papers. The day of the exam arrived. My stomach was twisted in knots and as I stared at the paper, some things seemed familiar. I came back home, felt okay about it.

The following two papers went good as well. Then came the math exam, the one that I had dreaded the most. As soon as I opened the paper, my mind went blank.

I barely managed to scribble over two pages, answering just a handful of questions, but there were 10-15 more pages to go. There was no way I could finish this. I couldn't make sense of anything written there. I felt completely lost and couldn't make heads or tails of it. Shit… this couldn't be happening. Not now, no… there was just one paper left after this. No! My parents would send me to boarding school. I didn't want to leave this house. No, no… I couldn't repeat this grade all over again. I tried to focus on the paper, but no matter how hard I tried, I couldn't understand a thing. Just give me something—anything—just to pass this test… the bare minimum. And then, just like that, the bell rang. That was it. I couldn't believe it was over. Yup, I was going to get shipped off to some other place.

I couldn't immediately go back home. I had to clear my mind first as I wasn't in the right senses. I went to a gaming café near my school. I must've been there for a good couple of hours. I looked at my watch and it was already past six.

"Shit! My mom is going to get so mad," I said to myself as I grabbed my back and left for my home.

I was walking up the slope, glancing at the sky—it was a bright yellow. Near the swings, I noticed a young lady pushing her toddler, who seemed to be enjoying it more than anything. I had the sudden urge to go over and tell them to hold onto this moment—to stay like this. This was the only time for pure joy. Enjoy it to the fullest while you're this young, because life is nothing but a bitter disappointment. Lost in this thought, a football suddenly rolled between my legs, nearly knocking me off balance. It looked old, probably dug out from some forgotten place, covered in mud stains and a greasy layer on top. In frustration, I kicked it hard toward the swings and kept walking.

I was too ashamed to talk to anyone. I went straight to home and locked myself in the room, tears filled my eyes. It was already pitch dark outside. I couldn't think straight. I started the tap, water gushing in at full swing. I splashed some water on my face, trying to calm myself down. I didn't know what to do. When a person has no idea what to do and is not in his right mind, he takes the worst possible decision that he could ever take. I opened my cupboard and pulled the sock drawer, there it lay in front of me my secret stash; and before I could control myself, I lit up a joint with the a matchstick and took a few puffs—just like that, in my uniform, in the open, not giving a damn in the world.

I sat down by the bedside, and after about ten minutes or so, it was over. My mind was still racing, but at least it felt a bit calmer than before. I lit a matchstick, sparked my next cigarette, and took a few puffs. Then, to my horror, the door slammed open, and there stood my father. He didn't say a word, but if looks could kill, I'd be dead on the spot. The death stare he gave me was chilling, and in a fit of anger, he slammed the door so hard it sent shivers down my spine. I was petrified. I just lay there, frozen, trying to make sense of what had just happened. I glanced at the piece of paper in my hand, too ashamed to even think about stepping outside.

My mom brought a plate of food to my room, but she was stone cold silent. She just kept the plate on the table and without uttering a single word, left the room. I managed only two bites. A pit formed in my stomach, growing until it seemed to swallow me whole. I was too embarrassed to go downstairs. I knew I was going to be shipped off as soon as school break started, and, oh yeah, first came the trip to the rehab center. Just to clarify, I was going to be sent to rehab to fight my so-called 'addiction' (God, I'd be stuck with junkies—people with bloodshot eyes, long, dirty fingernails, and no hope left in life). And after that? Off to boarding school, where I'd have to live alone with strangers—probably kids who had been kicked out of their homes too.

I would be served disgusting bowls of food every single day till I managed to get out of there. I would have to wake up at the crack of dawn, make my own bed, study the entire day and then that's it. That would be every single day of my life. That was a no-nonsense kind of place, barely talking to my parents maybe once or if I'm lucky maybe twice a week.

And that's if they even decided to talk to me. That was the 'perfect life' I had dreamed of. I couldn't stop spiraling. There were only two days left until my final paper, but what was the point? There was nothing left for me to do.

Even though this boy acted the way he did, I still feel a bit sad for him now. He spiraled completely out of control. He tried to salvage what was left, and he genuinely felt sorrow over what was happening. But in the end, he made the worst possible choice he could have in that situation.

This guy was surely done for. I wonder how he would fit in a boarding school and before that, a rehab! Things were about to get a hundred times worse. How could a guy who has had everything in his life, still be so sad and depressed. Judging by the looks of it, this boy was just creating problems for himself unlike people who have actual problems. Everything is in his control and if he wants to he can actually change his life, instead of just complaining and indulging in bad habits.

***

I didn't feel like living anymore and I couldn't take it anymore. What kind of life was this? There was nothing more that I could do… who in their right mind would want to live such a life. Like a madman, I started banging my head against the wall, tears streaming down my face. I was completely out of my senses. I couldn't think straight, and I definitely couldn't face my parents. In a fit of rage, I threw my schoolbooks across the room and tore apart old test sheets. What good were they to me now anyway? I was already flunking school.

I was so angry at myself, I trashed the entire room, dismantling my table, the entire bed, throwing my clothes all around, emptying out my cupboard. I just sat down in one corner, crying my eyes out. In anger, I got up and trampled over all of my stuff lying on the floor; my mind filled with rage. I tore a page from one of my notebooks and took out a pen.

I began writing a note in which I thanked my parents for everything they had done, but this was just too much for me to handle.

My hands quivered, causing ink to spill across the lines, while tears dropped onto the sheet, making it damp. I couldn't find more words to write on it and barely wrote even a paragraph. The last thing I said was, "This was entirely my decision; you all had nothing to do with it."

It was late in the evening, I passed by the other room and the door was shut. Mom and dad were in their room. I could hear the loud TV noise blaring throughout the entire house. I gathered up the courage and went towards the kitchen. The note in my left hand, almost crumpled in a sense. I opened one of the drawers and saw that all the cutlery that was stuffed inside: spoons, bowls, forks, knives, and plates.

I took out a knife and, without thinking twice, slit it straight across my wrists. By the time my mind grasped the gravity of what I had done, it was too late. Blood flowed out like a river, and the unimaginable pain coursed through me as I collapsed to the ground with a loud thump. Everything became blurry. I screamed at the top of my lungs! This was the worst decision, by far the stupidest I had ever made in my life—I didn't want to die... I didn't want to die... I didn't want to die... I wanted to live. I curled into a tight ball, screaming for help.

Withing minutes, I was soaked in a pool of blood as my eyes were filled with tears. This couldn't be it…what had just happened. I tried to drag my body across the kitchen floor, but the pain overcame me. I was paralyzed as I couldn't take control of my body anymore. It just refused to move. It had given up and to be honest, so had I. I couldn't believe I had actually let this happen. How stupid could a person be? I could hear hurried footsteps.

I thought I saw my mom's face, but at that moment, I wasn't sure if it was real or if I was hallucinating. I fought with all my might to stay conscious, but it felt nearly impossible. I was extremely dizzy, and the entire room was spinning. I heard faint voices of my parents calling in the background, but everything was a blur, too confusing for my overwhelmed mind to grasp. Amidst all the commotion, my eyes slowly closed.

I was stunned, unable to process the reality of what had just happened. Had the character really died? The shock and overwhelming sadness left me reeling. Even though I was desperate to find out what happened next, the weight of the moment was too much. I set the papers aside, feeling a deep, hollow ache. I collapsed into a restless sleep, my mind still spinning with the raw emotions of it all.

CHAPTER 6

RESTRICTIONS

The next day in school, I entered the classroom and we had Spanish test first thing in the morning. I looked around. A few along with me seemed prepared for the test but the rest of them nervous as usual. We were handed out the test papers and looking at it, it seemed fine. I got excited as I was able to answer all the questions and had just left one or two blanks empty.

Today was Friday—my favorite day of the week. There was always something special about it. The excitement of the weekend was in the air, knowing that there were two whole days of holiday lay ahead and we could wake up late and spend time at home.

Moreover, I would get a lot of time to read my father's novel. I was very curious to see what was going to happen next. I planned to finish a good chunk of it over the weekend. Dad had already booked movie tickets and we'd be eating out afterward. I quickly went back home from school being least bothered about Susan and Camille.

I opened the door to see mom was home early. Jason seemed a bit calmer, but he still wasn't talking to me. He had got a day pass and today was the one exception from his grounding, since it had been a while since the four of us had gone out together. With everyone so busy lately, today felt like it would be a much-needed break.

I swear, the one thing that I loved more than anything else in the world was the family outings that we had. They were extremely fun, exciting and we end up doing some of the most craziest things there were to do. To be honest, I think Mom and Dad needed these outings more than Jason and I did. They lived for this stuff. Whenever I talked to Mom, she'd share stories about the fun things she and Dad used to do together, and it seemed like they'd been making plans like this for a long time.

For instance, a couple of years before Jason was born, mom and dad both had entered a pie eating contest. They were no close to winning but dad apparently ate 11 pies (the winner had twenty) and I just couldn't believe it. This was the same man who would sometimes just eat fruits or salads because he 'had a heavy lunch that day.'

Last summer when all of us were on a vacation, we binged watched one of our favourite series finale for 20 hours straight in the living room. We pulled out a mattress, filled it with our favourite snacks and sat over there—just like that. The only time that we got up was for bathroom breaks. At one point, when mom got up to take an office phone call, we booed her a lot. That same summer, we visited one of the nearby cities in our locality. We did Go-Karting, indoor rock climbing and attended a magic show.

I'm really excited for this upcoming vacation time. Mom and dad said that the four of us would be travelling to Maui and take up surfing lessons for about a week or so. Both Jason and I were super pumped for it and so were our parents.

After some snacks, I headed to my practice. It was a lot of fun, but exhausting too. Once I finished, I hurried home, freshened up, and got ready for the movie. Dad had just gotten back, and we all set out together. Let me tell you, the movie was a blast! We grabbed slushies during the intermission, and before I knew it, it was over. I'd definitely watch it again in theaters if I could. Afterward, we had dinner at a nearby restaurant. The place was really beautiful.

The lighting was beautiful and the entire place was filled with warmth—yellow lights and soft music played in the background. This was really good considering the cold winds blowing outside; it was really cosy. Plus, the food was really good. We slurped on some hot chicken noodles. We were all starving, so we dug in while the steam was still rising from the bowls. Later, we ordered some delicious dumplings, dipping them into a sauce we thought was sweet—but to our surprise, it was mixed with wasabi!

We devoured the dumplings so quickly that by the time we realized it, our eyes were watering. That sauce was insanely spicy. All of our eyes turned red, and then Jason did the dumbest thing—he rubbed his eye with the same hand he'd used to eat. It made the burn so much worse! We were all literally crying but laughing at the same time. It was such a fun moment. We decided we desperately needed ice cream, so Dad picked some up as we headed home, our tongues hanging out of our mouths.

The three of us couldn't wait and ate the ice cream in the car to soothe our burning tongues, and it felt so much better. Poor Dad had to focus on driving, but Mom, sweet as ever, fed him a few bites while we crawled through traffic. Watching them made me feel so happy. Their love was so clear—in their talks, their laughter, their little arguments, and their gestures. Within minutes, we'd all finished our ice cream and were feeling a lot better.

We reached our home within half an hour, it was getting quite late. Even though I was tired and just wanted to sleep, I desperately wanted to read the book also. Once everyone had brushed their teeth and said goodnight, the house went dark. I waited for Jason to fall asleep, then quietly pulled out the stack of pages and switched on my reading light. Without hesitation, I dove straight into the story…

***

My head kept spinning and it took me a while to come back to my senses. Did I actually survive? I thought to myself. My vision was double, and it took about half an hour for it to clear up. Gradually, the fogginess lifted, and I began to make sense of my surroundings. My spine felt rigid, as if a rod had replaced my backbone. I tried to get up, but no matter how hard I tried, I couldn't move. Everything felt queasy, and I felt strangely different from my usual self.

In front of me lay a massive garden, with a myriad of flowers, plants, trees, a creekside view and everything. I realized I couldn't turn my head. I could not even feel my head. I couldn't understand what was going on and as I tried to move, I noticed that just below my eye level were a couple of leaves—yes, a couple of leaves—and it seemed as though they were stuck to me, as if they were a part of me.

My head started spinning. "No… it couldn't be… No, no…!" I kept muttering to myself, panic rising. "I must be dreaming. I just have to be… it couldn't be possible. Am I a plant??????"

I tried unfurling and folding my leaves, again and again. A hundred times, perhaps. It was no use. "Come on, wake up!" I pleaded, but nothing seemed to change. "Is this heaven? Or worse… is this hell??" My thoughts raced as I repeated, "No, no… nono… no…"

I attempted to laugh or smile, but it was impossible. "I can't feel my face… I can't feel anything!" I shouted in frustration. It felt like I was trapped in a cinder block, forced into it with no way out. "I can NEVER get out of this!" I cried out, despair consuming me.

My entire body felt rigid, it was the worst feeling imaginable. I couldn't distinguish anything. I couldn't feel my head; I was just looking straight, no left or right, nothing, just felt as if someone was holding me by the neck and forcing me to see ahead. I couldn't feel any of my limbs. Well I didn't have any. I wanted to cry, scream, "Please help me, look at me."

What?? Was this true?? I re-read the last line. Well, it seemed like it. I just continued to go on with it.

It felt as if I was forced into a wall that I barely fit into, with no room to shift my body, bound tight and unable to utter a word. The sensation was suffocating, and I felt like I would die on the spot. "What the hell is going on?" I thought in desperation. Just moments ago, I had been in my own house, in my kitchen, where I made the most painful and, frankly, the stupidest decision of my life. And now, I found myself in a place where I didn't even know if I was alive or dead.

"God knows what soul I'm trapped in," I lamented. I looked around at the familiar jogging tracks, their markers barely visible. I saw children riding their bikes, and everything seemed to blur together as I was carried deeper into the scene, unable to make sense of it all.

Everything seemed humongous in front of me, as if I had been shrunk to one fourth of my actual size. My vision had gone blurry. A couple of figures were moving in the background. Maybe children running around—yes, I could hear their faint voices from a distance. Some elders were taking their morning walk. I could see a plant right in front of me and it looked life-like, in fact it towered over me—casting a shadow.

I kept waiting for my vision to fade or for a voice to tell me to wake up. "How could I have been so foolish to kill myself?" I thought, overwhelmed by regret. "And what happened after that? How did I end up here, like this?"

A million thoughts raced through my head, and I didn't have answers for any of them. My body ached as I tried to keep a clear mind, but exhaustion took over, and I passed out.

I woke up in the middle of the night, glancing around. The darkness was absolute. I breathed rapidly, trying to calm myself. "Come on, move!" I muttered in frustration, but my body wouldn't cooperate. "Why can't I move? Am I superglued to the ground?" I exclaimed in pain.

This dream—or whatever it was—seemed endless. "It never stops," I thought in despair. "What am I supposed to do?" I lay there, helpless, waiting for this moment to pass. My body started to shut down as I remained in a state of utter perplexity.

The next morning, I woke up and my entire body seemed devoid of any energy. My vision was still blurry, and on top that I lacked even the basic strength. Suddenly, someone poured a stream of water over my head, jolting me into utter shock. However, that might have seemed to do the trick. After some time, my body began to respond better.

Every cell absorbed the much-needed water. As I managed to get a grasp on the situation, a huge insect came right in front of me. I tried to shoo it away with all my might, but I couldn't manage to do much. It danced around me and vanished after a bit.

"Huh! This is pretty much it, I guess. I have reached hell, and this is my punishment—I have to live the rest of my life as a plant? Some strange version of hell, I guess," I thought.

I was taken aback as I looked over the entire place. I could see the pond—damn! It was the same very one from my past life. A wave of nostalgia washed over me, pulling me back to an incident from a couple of years ago when I was around ten. and I was brought back to that incident. Mom had brought me to this garden, and I had carried my baseball and glove with me. We played together for a while, but sensing she was getting tired, I took the ball and glove and decided to stroll by myself.

In the middle of the garden was a small pond. Not realizing how far I had walked, I turned to look back. Oof! I had ventured quite a distance. I threw the ball into the air as high as I could and scrambled to catch it, running left and right. For about fifteen minutes, I repeated this over and over again.

Out of nowhere, a group of boys that seemed to be a few years elder than me, maybe in the tenth grade or so appeared. They were just strolling, laughing and in their own world. All of a sudden, while running to catch the ball, I bumped into them hard and I fell on the ground, pushing two of them backwards with me.

"Hey fatty, watch where you're going," one of them shouted.

As I tried to get up, I began to apologize but I guess I just got a little scared with the incident.

"Ssss sso…sooo," I stuttered, trying to say sorry.

Their annoyance grew, and one of them gave me a hard shove. I crashed to the ground, landing painfully on my left butt cheek. "Oww!" I winced, the pain searing through me.

Desperately, I looked around, trying to retrieve my glove and ball. But before I could reach them, one of the boys kicked the ball away with his foot. "Hey! That's mine!" I protested, but my voice was barely audible over their jeering. I tried to get the things back, but they just started tossing it around to one another. I tried to reach it, but I just couldn't. They were much taller than me and I really couldn't jump that high.

"Maybe stop hogging on the burger and cakes and you can get your stuff back," one of them said.

I tried to plead and tried my level best to reach them, but I just couldn't reach them. While they just continued to tease me and mock me and finally after I gave up and just stood at one place. Tears were about to roll down my eyes.

"Awww.. alright hear you go," he said, and he lowered his

hand down with the ball and the glove.

I reached to take it and he just pulled his hand back. Then, without warning, he hurled them straight ahead. I watched in horror as the ball and glove sailed through the air, landing with a loud splash in the pond.

"Score!" one of the boys shouted, grinning, and the others burst into laughter.

They turned away, still laughing and talking loudly, leaving me standing there, fists clenched in helpless rage. My entire body shook as tears streamed down my cheeks. I took a deep breath, choking back a sob, and walked towards the pond to retrieve my things.

When I reached the edge, I saw them—my baseball and glove—floating in the murky water, completely soaked. I removed my shoes and socks, dipping my feet into the freezing water. The stench was overwhelming, and the cold sent shivers up my spine. Still, I leaned forward to grab them, but just as I reached out, my leg got caught on something beneath the surface. Before I knew it, I plunged face-first into the water, the icy splash drenching my entire body.

I scrambled to my feet, shivering uncontrollably, my clothes heavy with the cold, filthy water.

I was brought back to my realization by a high-pitched sound. A strange sensation washed over my body. My body seemed to absorb some tiny gas molecules that were released in the air. I became alert, felt that something was not right.

"Was I getting some communication from another plant," I thought.

At first, I struggled to make out the figures huffing and puffing toward me, and then I saw them—a pack of dogs.

"Wait, what's that noise?" I thought, panic rising within me.

The dogs looked so gigantic—the size of a monster. Never had I felt that dogs could be so dangerous. Some of them were tearing up the other plants, chewing up their leaves and completely disfiguring them clumsily making their way through the place. I just prayed that they would go away without touching and thankfully enough they did.

Many of the plants were left in tatters, their leaves shredded and their beauty destroyed.

As the beam of sunlight bathed the entire garden, I began to feel better. More energy was being absorbed, and I could sense each cell of mine using the stored water and minerals. After about an hour or so, I felt completely revitalized.

The rest of the day passed normally, but standing in one spot was incredibly tiring and frustrating. I couldn't begin to express how much I missed being human. If I could, I'd leap around, jump, prance, dive, and roll all over this very garden. As the sun began to set, the temperature dropped, and the dark layers of night wrapped around everything. My body grew weary, and before I knew it, I was drifting into a deep sleep.

All of a sudden, the same weird feeling arose again. The same one that I had felt when all the dogs were approaching. It meant only one thing—danger was near. As I looked up, the sky appeared like a vast black bowl, threatening to engulf the earth. Thunder rumbled loudly, making me shiver at the sound. The winds howled fiercely, and what had started as a gentle drizzle quickly turned into a torrential downpour.

How I longed to escape from this place—anywhere but

here. Oh, how I missed my comforting bed and the warm cup of milk Mom always brought me before bedtime. I would have given anything to be there right now, far from this chaos. Meanwhile, the rain showed no signs of letting up. I began to sway uncontrollably from side to side, unable to stop. It felt as if I was being dragged about by the fury of nature itself. The wind's howling grew more intense, and I started to feel a sharp, biting pain in my body.

I tilted my view and, to my horror, saw that part of my roots had come loose. I wanted to scream at the top of my lungs, but no sound emerged. The scene around me was one I would never forget: plants were completely uprooted, mud was scattered everywhere, and even the towering trees were swaying violently, with some on the brink of toppling over.

I was being pulled and dragged, with only one last root still clinging to the ground. My body was almost completely exposed. I looked up at the sky, desperately hoping this nightmare would end.

Suddenly, the final root holding me in place gave way. I collapsed to the ground, and the pain that surged through me was beyond anything I had ever felt. I lay there, my body going numb, and as my vision started to fade, I realized with a sinking feeling that it was over for me.

What just even happened. The boy, who had once been alive, was now a plant? I read the section again, trying to piece together everything. My mind was spinning with confusion. Had he really turned into a plant? Was this all a dream? How could he have become a plant when he had killed himself in the previous part? Everything seemed so disorienting. I flipped the page, hoping for clarity.

I imagined that poor plant getting tugged from the ground and trying to withhold it, but the ferocious storm was just too much for it to handle. The entire atmosphere seemed dark and gloomy. I flipped the page to see what happened next…

CHAPTER 7

SHAME

My head pounded with pain as I slowly regained consciousness. I was flat on my back, staring at a stark white ceiling. To my horror, a giant spider was creeping toward me, and I fainted again. When I woke up, I saw my own tentacles and screamed. I forced myself to look in the mirror, only to find a horrifying sight: my body was dark brown with grotesque tentacles and eight black eyes below my head.

"This can't be real," I thought desperately. "It's just a hallucination." Despite my efforts to convince myself otherwise, I couldn't escape the nightmare. I crawled away from the mirror, unable to bear my hideous reflection, while my vision remained disoriented and unclear.

What was even happening. This guy had been turned into a plant and now, he was turned into this horrible creature. I needed a break. I closed the book and went outside for a bit. I slouched off and fell asleep.

The next morning was busy as usual. I got dressed quickly, ate some peanut butter and jelly sandwiches and left for school. Today luckily, one of the teachers were absent so all of my friends and I made paper airplanes and were flying them within the classroom. The class boys were running inside and jumping across tables; basically a complete circus!

Seeing this commotion and laughter, I remembered one of my friends. Her name was Ava and she and I were the closest of friends. Her dad got relocated last summer and they shifted. She and I would always share this lovely choco-oreo milkshake that would be available at the shop just outside our school.

Anyway, I was brought back to the real world by the ringing of the school bell. The rest of the day was pretty much the same. I sat and completed my work, had my dinner, and then all the house lights were shut off.

I pulled out the novel and continued to read…

***

My body was permanently hunched, parallel to the floor, with four hind legs balancing me and four front legs guiding my direction. It was confusing to manoeuvre with eight legs instead of two. I stumbled and tripped at first, but after 10-15 minutes, I mastered the movement, each leg moving in sync and adjusting to my weight.

I reached the end of the platform and saw a large white dome-shaped structure beside me. There was no visible way to cross it, and a massive wall loomed on the other side. The ceiling seemed distant, and behind me was a gigantic mirror.

In front of me seemed the doorway and I as turned around a huge bar of lump was placed on a slightly raised platform. I moved towards it slowly and tried to climb up but suddenly felt a slimy wet thing. The lump was extremely slimy and slippery at the same time. It was a bar of soap! The huge dome structure was the wash basin. This entire place is someone's bathroom!!!

I tried placing one leg on the side of the wall. I could feel that I could balance on the wall. I placed another leg and it amazed me. Letting go, the rest of my body clung to the wall. I was defying gravity.

I could feel my head spinning as my eyes faced the looming ceiling far away. I slowly tried to rotate my body across the wall's surface—removing one leg at a time.

I just hoped I wouldn't fall—I would for sure die on the spot. Slowly but steadily, I faced the ground. I stretched a leg downward and took a cautious step. "Woah!" This was one of the craziest moments of my life—like being Spider-Man! Step by step, I crawled downward, nervous that I'd fall at any second. Finally, I reached the floor, my body back in position.

My head was spinning from this stunt. I crawled over to the end of the floor and lay there. I found a small crack near the end – it was in the shape of a cave. I felt it could be a good resting spot. I had a feeling it was nighttime. I crawled into the crack and rested over there. I could feel my heartbeat slowing down, feeling exhausted.

It was my body trying to tell me to take some rest now. My legs curled up naturally, and for the first time, I felt a strange comfort in this grotesque new body. Maybe this is how spiders sleep, I thought. I could stay here for hours. But eventually, I forced myself to move.

Stretching out my legs, I scanned the room. The only way forward was across the bathroom floor, but what next? Should

I try to leave? What if someone saw me and squashed me on sight?

Just as I was caught in this dilemma, the bathroom door suddenly burst open with a deafening slam. It crashed against the wall just inches from me. My heart nearly exploded. I stood frozen in place, paralyzed with fear. Another inch, and I would have been a goner.

Was I nuts to think that I would be able to go outside on my own. I wouldn't survive two minutes along with these Godzillas—known as human beings. Luckily the human couldn't see me as I was covered by the basin. An enormous foot slammed onto the floor, shaking the entire ground.

The lights turned bright on as I stood frozen on the spot. A massive foot stepped inside, followed by the loud slam of the door shutting behind it. The entire floor shock from the force. I was too scared to even twitch. The tap turned on, loud noise and water flowed across at full force.

Without making a sound, I started crawling up the wall and eventually hung upside down beneath the basin, clinging to its underside. Everything about this situation was terrifying, but strangely, hanging like this felt almost normal now.

Hung there beneath the basin, my mind drifting back to the life I had before—when I was human. Regret weighed heavily on me, even more than the strange new body I was trapped in. How could I have been so careless, so oblivious to the simple joys of living?

I used to complain about the smallest things—walking for too long, aching feet after a day out, or the rain ruining my plans. I never cherished the feel of the sun on my skin or the freedom to move, to run. I had legs that could carry me anywhere I wanted, hands that could grasp and create, eyes that could see the world in all its beauty. Yet, I never appreciated any of it. Not really.

Now, I was reduced to this—skittering on eight legs, crawling along surfaces, stuck in a body that wasn't mine. The little things that annoyed me before? I would give anything to have them back. The warmth of a cup of coffee, the comfort of a soft bed, the simple pleasure of lying down after a long day. I never realized how lucky I was.

I could only imagine the pain my parents must be feeling. Their only child, gone because I couldn't see a way out of my own darkness. They had given me everything—love, support, and countless sacrifices. How had I repaid them? By abandoning them with nothing but unanswered questions and endless grief. The thought of their faces, their tears, their anguish—haunted me more than the new body I was forced to inhabit.

The man was now brushing his teeth. I could hear the loud noise of the bristles being brushed against his teeth. It's so strange how much a spider can notice, even to the smallest details. Then rinsed his mouth and gargled a couple of times. All this time, I lay there silently as I stared at his hairy legs. He then completed all his routine work, went over to the toilet and sat down.

Ohhh no!!!! I didn't want to see this view at all. I turned around and began to crawl in the opposite direction.

I crawled down slowly and stayed close to the end of the wall. After what seemed like an eternity, I could hear the deafening noise of the jet spray and finally the man got up, pulled his trousers up and headed to the sink. He washed his hands and went out of the bathroom, switching off the light.

"Pffff! Finally… that was intense," I muttered to myself.

I was very nervous after the entire incident. If I had to survive, I would have to stay inside this bathroom for the rest of the time. My stomach rumbled with an impatient growl—oh no, it seemed I'd have to leave this bathroom after all.

What do spiders eat, anyway? A tingling sensation swept over me, hinting at something nearby. As I carefully navigated the space, I spotted a massive structure that resembled a bed. It was the storeroom. I stepped or rather crawled inside it. The sight that greeted me was overwhelming: boxes were stacked haphazardly, creating a labyrinth of clutter. Old suitcases and cricket bats lay scattered among the piles. The room was packed to the brim, with boxes of old clothes reaching up to the ceiling.

No one seemed to be around. I looked around but couldn't find any food. A couple of flies seemed to be in the room. A huge craving for food filled my mind and all I could think was eating the flies only.

What kind of miserable state was I in, thinking about eating flies? The thought of it should have brought up disgust, but I felt nothing except hunger. I guess I am losing touch with my human side, if I haven't already.

Oh no! His mind is clearly not in the right senses. I mean, whose wouldn't be, after experiencing what he has experienced? Someone get him out of all this and back to the place where he belongs…

I looked around and crawled across the other way, looking to see what my options were. The flies seemed to be moving zigzag all the way, everyway. They zoomed past me and flew out from the crack of the open door. Well, there goes my food. I looked in awe and couldn't find anything else nearby.

Hunger pangs returned, stronger than before—a sense of hunger that had to be satisfied. I looked around and near one of the old suitcases were a couple of red ants that seemed to be in a little hurry. I hid behind a box, to ensure they do not see me. As they came near, I attacked them, but they were too quick to respond and immediately began to skedaddle. They split ways and I went behind one, leaving the others at peace. I crawled with all my might and at the fastest pace possible. The ant was a pain in the ass.

Crawling with all my strength, I chased the ant across the room. It was relentless, forcing me to cover almost the entire space before I was finally within a leg's reach. With a swift strike of my fang, I pierced through the ant's body, and a sticky, transparent liquid oozed out.

The place seemed very familiar to me and even though I tried my best to remember, for the life of me, I couldn't remember it. But there was something eerily familiar about it. More than the other rooms, this seemed extremely familiar, and I don't know why.

The ant was wounded badly and after a few seconds of squirming around, trying to fight for life, it stopped moving completely. Just like that, it was dead. I had to eat this thing now. Even the thought seemed repulsive and yucky in the mind, my body seemed to crave for it. I cut open the parts and piece by piece, began to devour it. I closed my eyes, biting and swallowing, trying to ignore the conflicting sensations of taste and disgust.

After some time, I was done and without looking back,

I crawled away from that spot. It didn't completely fill my stomach but at least it eased the craving. The experience made me think about how tough hunting for food is. How was it that spiders could hunt so many preys and yet want more, over and over? I barely managed to catch one ant and that too after a long cat and mouse chase. All of this made me question my choices once again. But, now I had nothing but regret.

I had turned into a spider and yet after learning so much, I still hadn't utilized the greatest weapon of the spider—the one that's the spider's own identity, its own silk. I backed into a corner, laid down, looked at my abdomen and from one leg, pulled out a sticky thread of silk from a cone-shaped gland on my abdomen. It flew out and landed on the floor. Ahhh! Now things were getting interesting!

One of my hind legs managed to pull the woven thread while I crawled with the others. Being upside down had become my new normal, as if I had been doing this all my life. I still got scared when I came across the bathroom mirror; seeing my own reflection made me want to throw up. I preferred to avoid the mirror. Although I had mastered the drag line, it was exhausting. I had to stop midway, taking a break while dangling in the air. Suddenly, a large, hairy man entered the bathroom, swinging the door open.

"Why can't these humans just sleep?" I screamed in my spider voice.

I was literally in the middle of my dragline when I had paused for a break. A huge towel was dropped over his shoulder. He had come in to take a bath. Okk..okk, I had to skedaddle from here as fast as I can. I tried going back up and before he could come near the shower, I was at the ceiling.

He undressed and then stepped forward. He switched on the shower, droplets began to pour, followed by a jet stream of water that destroyed my drag line, sending it cascading away with the current.

A little part of it remained at the top. Never mind; all I had to ensure was to get out of this area and that too in one piece. I crawled down the side of the shower, making good progress. The light brown, textured bathroom wall helped me blend in and provided some cover. I had managed to descend halfway when he suddenly noticed me.

All of a sudden, the man's steely eyes glanced at me with a look of disgust.

"YUCK!! he bellowed, his loud voice echoing through the bathroom."

The hair on my entire body stood up. I was completely frozen with that word. I looked back at him. He had piercing dark brown eyes, round chubby cheeks and what seemed to be a full set of thick black hair. But all I could see was pure hatred; eyes that could kill.

Quickly, he cupped his hands, collected some water, and poured it down on me. The entirety came crashing down on me. It hit me with such a force, I slipped from the wall and went down a few inches. Just as I managed to get my firm grip back on the wall, another flow of water came crashing down, hitting me so hard from the behind, making me lose my balance again. I slipped a few inches and almost fell to the ground. I moved away as quickly as I could, escaping the shower area. I felt extremely tired curled up underneath the toilet and began to rest.

I straightened my legs after what I'm assuming to be a

couple of hours. The entire room was quiet again. The loud voice of that men rang in my ears once again. I felt completely embarrassed by that word and felt a new low today. I had never felt like this before. It was a strange, unsettling feeling that could get on someone's nerves. Nevertheless, I began to crawl at the top of the bathroom floor, suddenly, a clump of dust fell from above. I moved away to dodge it and came face to face with a scary looking spider.

"Perfect," I muttered with fear.

I tried to shriek, but no sound came out. I lost my balance and crashed into the sink. The spider was just my reflection. I had always been afraid of spiders, and now, I had become one—a creature that people would squash without a second thought. I was bruised and devastated, reduced to a mere arachnid, feared and loathed for my appearance.

I stared at my reflection, trying to look away but failing. "This can't be me," I muttered. The black, soulless eyes blinked back at me, surrounded by a round, sluggish brown body, sharp fangs at the mouth, and spindly legs that crept from every side. "I'm disgusting," I whispered, feeling a wave of revulsion. "How did it come to this?"

My stomach growled, snapping me out of my thoughts. "Oh great, now I'm hungry," I grumbled. "Guess I need to build a web. How do spiders even do that?" I crawled up to the top corner of the bedroom. "Alright, let's do this."

I began creating a vertical drag line from the ceiling. "Just a bit more," I told myself as I slowly pulled the silk. Moving to the side, I started connecting the ends to form a horizontal line. "This is harder than it looks," I sighed, struggling to hold everything in place.

Piece by piece, I formed the circular web in the middle. "I never imagined making a web would be so tiring," I muttered, feeling the exhaustion creep in.

Once the web was finished, I hung there, panting. "Now I just wait... for some unlucky fly to wander into my trap," I whispered, trying to ignore the gnawing hunger that was slowly building.

I spent hours building the web, moving in a slow, circular pattern until it finally took shape. "Not bad for a first attempt," I whispered, though the structure wobbled in places. Still, it was something. I just hoped it would bring me food.

The days blurred together, following the same dull routine. I'd hide when the hairy man came into the bathroom, waiting for him to leave so I could crawl around in peace. Exploring the storeroom turned up nothing—no food, no insects, just endless searching.

I grew tired, frustrated. "How long can I survive without food?" I wondered as I lay in the shadows, my hunger gnawing at me. Weeks had passed, and my web remained empty. The darkness, which once felt comforting, now felt like a trap. Each flicker of light brought a small hope, only to be crushed when nothing flew into my web.

"I can't keep going like this," I muttered. I felt weak, desperate. If I didn't find food soon, I would starve. Time was running out.

Eww… in my mind I could imagine a spider and trust me, everyone who I knew in this world would hate a spider. Just looking at it was absolutely revolting. Until a few years ago, I would scream at the top of my lungs and jump around whenever I saw a spider. I have just started gaining some courage and would kill it with a slipper or whatever was handy nearby. That's one of the reasons I started wearing slippers. Why couldn't have he become something better? This was surely torture..

***

I *looked around but couldn't find a single thing to eat. In front of me stood a door. "Okay, once I go in, there's no turning back, no matter what's on the other side."*

I scuttled frantically through the room, my web torn and useless. The constant harassment and failed attempts at food had left me weak and desperate. I had to find something—anything—to make my existence bearable. I ventured beyond the bathroom, my legs trembling as I crawled across the floor in search of a new hiding spot or a better vantage point.

The door seemed shut; only revealing a tiny gap, yet big enough for me to fit inside. I squeezed myself in it. I was inside the other room. This one was completely different than the previous one. It was a bedroom. I was exploring the room and suddenly a huge foot nearly flattened me. I darted aside, narrowly escaping the crushing weight of a teenage girl, around 14 to 16 years old. On the other side of the room, a younger girl, perhaps 10 or 12, was seated on the bed.

She had frizzy hair and was wearing a pink t-shirt and pink shorts. I decided to get out of here but as soon as I was about to, the elder one's eyes matched mine. Her eyes widened in horror. "Ew!" she screamed, her voice echoing with a piercing intensity. She took out her slipper, and hurled it towards me. I didn't need to be told twice, I made a run for it. I scrambled up the side of the wall, moving as quickly as my spider legs could carry me.

The slipper smacked the adjacent wall with a deafening thud. I continued to move in a zigzag motion, dodging the attacks coming from all sides. I managed to climb the celling, from this new vantage point, spotted a small crack in the wall.

"This is my chance to save my life," I thought to myself.

The young girl couldn't understand where I had gone. The other one just sat on her side of the bed, perplexed by what had just happened. The elder one searched for me for another minute or so and eventually gave up. The two of them were preparing to go to bed. I looked outside the window, and it seemed dark outside. The hate that I got from these people was unimaginable.

Two seconds of a glance, and people were after me and what for? Did I cause them any harm? Nope. Did I steal any of their food? Nope. Did I trouble any of their belongings? Nope. Simply because I was hideous and scary to look at. I felt completely insulted and embarrassed by this incident. From a boy who had everything in his life, I had been reduced to a pile of garbage.

It must've been their time to sleep. But maybe one good thing came out of this place. I leered at the other side near the wardrobe, where not one, but an army of ants was present. It was time to feast. Finally, some relief after these weeks of torture. I waited for the lights to go off and began to plan my attack. While I was planning my attack, all of a sudden it hit me.

I have been in this place. I have been here once. I could now remember it as clear as day. No wonder that younger girl's face seemed so familiar. It was around sixth or seventh grade I think so. I'm not too sure. It was this girl Alice's birthday and she had invited the entire class to come. I wasn't too keen on going. I usually avoided meeting everyone else as much as I could, but mom had forced me to go for it. I showed up at around half past two. All the others were in the hall. I looked around. No one really came up to me, so I just sat in the corner.

I think Alice's mother was also at home the time, but she had to go out for an hour or so. All of us decided to play hide and seek. Initially everyone wanted me to become the denner, but I didn't mind. I was just happy to play the game. After around 15 minutes or so of playing and searching everyone (the house was really massive, and it was impossible to find anyone) I finally caught one person.

When it was my turn to hide, I remember a couple of boys were trying to find a place to hide.

"'You know what we should do," one whispered.

"What?" I replied.

"We should go and hide in the storeroom that's on the above floor. There is no way that we would ever get caught.." the boy replied. We decided to go up and when we opened the storeroom door, it seemed dusty inside. It was pitch dark.

"Why don't you just turn on the light from inside and we'll join you," one of them said.

I slowly stepped inside the place and as I was trying to find the light switch, I heard the door shut with a loud bang and then heard a click. I tried opening the door from the inside, but they had LOCKED IT from the outside.

"HEY….IT'S NOT FUNNY… LET ME OUT…. LEEETTT MEEE OUTTTTTT," I shouted at the top of my voice. But they just giggled, laughed, and ran from there.

I started banging the door with my fist, but no one heard me. I eventually did manage to turn the lights on. It was more or less the same stuff – boxes and boxes everywhere, some empty suitcases, and most of it, everything was dusty.

I kept shouting from the inside, but no one seemed to hear me. For nearly two hours, I was trapped in that place. Finally, Alice's mom heard me. When she opened the door, her face froze in shock. She looked at me and asked, "What happened? Why are you in here?" But I didn't answer. I just ran out, tears streaming down my face, straight into the hall. Most of the guests had already gone home. Mom was there, waiting for me, and I ran into her arms, unable to hold back my sobs.

She kept asking me to explain, and when I finally told her everything, she was furious. She didn't hold back, giving Alice's mom a piece of her mind before taking me home.

If spiders could cry, I'd be in tears right now. But I suppose creatures like me don't get the luxury of emotions. Disgusting and emotionless—that's what we are. Anyway, enough of that. It was time to focus on my plan. There was no point in lingering on the past. The room was now pitch dark, except for a few dim spots illuminated by the outside light.

I made my move, crawling silently, upside down, as the room lay still before me.

Carefully, laying each step on the ceiling, I began to move slowly towards the other side. Both the girls had fallen asleep, and it was the perfect opportunity. I steadied myself as I held my breath, cautiously moving towards my prey. I looked from afar, but it had become extremely difficult to spot them. I inched closer and closer in that direction and was soon on the other side. I scanned the entire area, and yes, there it was—a puny little red ant carrying on with his daily work as he kept moving down the wardrobe side.

I began to create a drag line and slowly and steadily lowered myself towards it. Right below me was the younger girl, peacefully napping and enjoying her stress-free life. As I neared the ant, I felt a sudden pull and immediately looked towards the top. To my horror, the silk thread had stretched to the extreme and was on the verge of snapping. I dangled in midair, trying to stabilize myself and regain focus. I had to reach for the wall or someplace where I could get a grip. The thread pulled even further, now just a second away from splitting in two.

I tried to get near the side of the wall and bam, it split into two. I fetl the sudden loss of balance and just fell—not just fell, but straight onto the young girl's face. As I hit the surface, I immediately saw her eyes pop wide open. Her mouth let out a scream as she jumped out of bed and began frantically leaping across the room. A flying hand came at me with full force, slapping me straight across the floor. She kept screaming at the top of her lungs until the entire house was awake.

As I hit the floor, I felt tremendous pain, mainly due to the brute force of the flying palm. I tried to stand up with all my might, but I couldn't. I lay flat on the ground. And then, that hairy middle-aged man entered the room. After him came a plump woman, maybe in her mid 40s or so. That small girl was practically crying at this point, and she pointed at me with utter disgust.

"Oh, this thing's still alive," bellowed the man.

I didn't want to die like this. All I wanted was some food to fill my stomach. Please leave me alone. What did I ever do to you.

I tried to move away, dragging my half-damaged body across the floor. Meanwhile, the slipper was already in his hand. He threw it with all his might, straight at me. It came flying and crushed my entire body into pieces.

I couldn't describe the pain that shot up through my entire body as I lay there. My body was crushed, sticky liquid poured out onto the ground. My breathing slowed, and my legs twitched for the very last time. The entire room began to dissolve around me. I lost consciousness, and it was pitch dark once again.

Woah! What the helllll.... Ewww. I could actually imagine that ugly spider from up close, as if it was me who turned into a life-sized spider. I would literally faint if I saw a life size spider. Wow, this entire experience felt like a roller coaster. I looked at the writing and could almost feel the pain the character went through. How horrible it must be to life such a life—a life of disgust and hatred. The sole fact that people would run away from you at your very sight is revolting. It was such a strange feeling. I actually felt bad for the spider.

Life just wasted away like that. If this taught me anything, it was to love yourself and not stress about the way you look. Dressing nice and taking care of oneself is one thing but judging people on their looks is just cruel. Even the kids in my class are just mean what it comes to such things. I actually just felt sad after reading all of this. I shut the book and turned off the lights—the same chapter playing in my head as I drifted off to sleep.

The next day, I woke up quite late and not having anything much to do, I figured I would read my book.

There was no homework this weekend, only one day of practice and mom and dad were going to be busy. So, I had a lot of time to kill.

After breakfast, mom and dad both left for work. I worked on my assignments that were given to us from school. I spent a lot of my day listening to music and just painting away. Time just flew by. It was already time for lunch. One of my favourite chicken burritos were kept in the fridge. After I devoured that with my favourite episode of 'Gilmore Girls' I sat back again with my painting. I put on my headphones, and I began to paint again. I was completing this beautiful landscape with the forests in the background and the night sky shimmering above. By the time I looked up from my desk, it was already dark. I started the television and was just flipping channels for the fun of it.

Jason had gone out again—I think to a friend's place, for some work, or something. He came back late evening and by that time, even mom and dad were back home—super tired. After eating dinner, all of us were ready to jump into our respective beds. I switched off the lights, but sleep evaded me. I was twisting and turning but for some reason, I couldn't fall asleep. I looked around and my eyes fell on the same stack of sheets. I switched on my reading light and continued from where I'd left.....

CHAPTER 8

SURVIVAL

I opened my eyes, only to be blinded by the sun's sharp rays piercing my skin. I let out a soft screech, but a very high-pitched sound came out of my throat.

'Uh oh! What in God's name had I turned into now,' I thought.

Lying flat on my back, I blinked as my vision adjusted, and tall, swaying grasses came into focus. I tried to move, lifting what I thought was my arm—only to see a light-brown, thin leg with a hoof at the end. Oh no. No, no, no! I scrambled to my feet—or rather, to my fours—as panic began to settle in. My heart raced as I attempted to walk, my legs wobbling beneath me. Everything felt surreal, and my blurred vision only added to the confusion.

A massive area of grass revealed itself. The sun was hitting the ground with all its force, covering each and every spot and illuminating each and every piece of grass. There seemed to be areas and patches of grass stretching endlessly. I could manage to see some blurry images which I'm guessing were trees, right till the very end.

I scanned the horizon, hoping for some sign of familiarity, some marker to tell me where I was or how I had gotten here. But there was nothing. Just the same unchanging landscape in every direction—a never-ending field of grass and trees. My heart sank. The road ahead, this vast open world, felt like a trap. A cage made not of bars, but of the endless, oppressive sameness that surrounded me.

No one seemed to be around, at least not anywhere near. In the far distance, I could make out some faint, shifting shapes, but they were too far away to identify. My head felt unnaturally heavy as I took in the scene around me, weighed down by the weight of reality sinking in.

I looked and spotted a mighty tree nearby. I began walking towards if. It felt so weird travelling like this, on all fours, yet better off than those previous eight ones. My hooves clipped clopped with each step. I stumbled, not noticing the gap. There was no proper road or a straight path to walk ahead. The entire place around me was just an entirety of 'ups and downs' filled with rocks and cracks and carcass. Finally, I reached the tree, the dry crunch of a leaf beneath my hooves, the only sign of life in this desolate place.

At least this would do for the time being. Exhausted, I laid down and rested against its gigantic bark and was feeling quite better already. The searing sun still blazed overhead, but at least here, under the tree's shadow, I found a moment of respite. The grass looked like it hadn't seen water for weeks. The scorching heat was already starting to make me thirsty. I couldn't find any pond nearby. I decided that my best option was to rest against this cooling bark.

Before I knew it, my eyes were shut, and I drifted into deep thought. After what seemed like a couple of hours, I slowly opened one of my eyes and I could see a small hazy figure at a distance. I got a very strong musky smell from that same direction. I couldn't really make out what it was, so I stood up and edged a bit closer in that direction. My vision cleared up and I could see what seemed to be the most magnificent pair of antlers that I had ever seen.

The rugged brown complexion made it look rustic. They looked weathered yet powerful, like they could slice through the toughest obstacles. There was something mystical about them, their slender form hiding a deeper strength. I wondered what my own antlers must look like. Surely, they were massive too, given the weight I felt pressing down on my head.

Just as I was lost in thought, the creature finally emerged from behind the slope. It was docile, with pointy, rounded ears standing upright, and a mane of soft pastel shades draped over its neck. Its sleek, dark brown body was speckled with freckles of white. Its thin, delicate legs moved gracefully as its tail swayed behind. It stopped, standing still, facing away from me, yet its head was turned in my direction, eyes locked onto mine.

I wasn't sure how to react. Those deep, black, beady eyes simply stared at me. I straightened myself, trying to appear calm and confident. I didn't want to scare it away—or worse, show fear. Slowly, I took a step toward it. Still, it didn't move. I took another, our gaze unbroken.

Suddenly, the creature let out a strange but loud sound, almost like a signal or call to someone unseen. Then it looked back at me, its expression now softer, more inviting. Its tail began to wag slowly, as if it had decided I was no longer a threat.

WOAHHH, damn.... This person's travelling from

one life to another. Hopping from species to species. This kind of imagination was something truly different. Hats off to my dad! Never expected this story to go in this way. So this guy was now going to spend his life in this sweaty jungle! Eating other animals and grass and whatnot. Eww! What if there was no way out? He must be regretting his decision so much.

Suddenly, I could see about maybe fifty or so, more of these deer slowly walking towards me. What a sight it was, each one moving in a similar manner yet having some distinct quality. Some of them had antlers, some didn't. Some antlers were massive – grown about till two or three meters and some were so very tiny. Hardly about a stint on the head. They all moved in groups, even as they approached this place.

There were some very cute baby deer nudging along their parents, sticking very close and walking in their comfort. They crossed the area and were now all around me. Meanwhile, the deer that had been keeping a close watch on me came a bit closer, made a grunting sound. I too tried my level best to replicate it and managed to produce the same sound. However, it came out a bit different.

Nevertheless, I looked around and was feeling extremely hungry, and judging by the behaviour of the others, they too were feeling the same. The sun was at its absolute peak, and we needed some shade as well. All the deer began to move forward in search of some greenery that could be of some use to us. As they began to move ahead, the deer that was close to me, nudged me, indicating for me to come along. I didn't have to be asked twice. It was better for me to be along with the group instead of me trying to make it out on my own. I wouldn't survive even a day in this blazing piece of crap, surrounded by nothing but an endless stretch of land, grass, rocks and hills.

I began to move along with the other deers as they went ahead. Most of them walked in an organized manner, a single line with only a few meters distance between them. Some of them walked around in search of food or water. The other few playfully ran alongside the elder ones, they seemed to be the children; not too young, but not old enough to be called adults. Other baby deer were walking right alongside the parents, underneath their shadow with a relaxed expression on their faces.

Seeing them brought tears to my eyes as memories of my own family flooded my mind. What must they have gone through when they saw my body lying lifeless on the kitchen floor? I couldn't bear to imagine the expressions on their faces—the shock, the grief. What must they have felt? What must they have thought? Even though there were so many moments when I was furious with them, moments when I wanted to leave and never come back, I could never truly stay away. When I found out I was being sent to a boarding school, I felt completely abandoned, like I was being exiled from the only place I belonged. The thought of being separated from the only people who truly cared for me was unbearable.

A sharp grunt from the deer beside me snapped me back to the present. The walk felt endless. My legs were starting to tire, and every step felt heavier than the last. But we had no choice—everywhere we looked, there was only dried-up grass, nothing edible. The sky had turned gloomy, casting a gray shadow over everything, and the sun was dipping towards the horizon, painting the sky in shades of orange and red.

After what seemed like hours of trudging through the barren land, something caught our attention—finally glimmer of hope. In the distance, there was a pond-like area. Excitement rippled through the group, and we hurried towards it. But as we got closer, our hopes were crushed. The pond was nearly dried up, cracked mud stretched across most of its surface, with water next to nothing.

How will we survive in this heat. I had no idea, but I knew one thing. Life is full of struggles, but we just have to stay strong and that is what I did.

As I reached the edge of the pond, I bent down to drink, but something made me pause. I caught sight of my reflection in the water—a face I hadn't truly seen until now.

My eyes were piercing black in colour, surrounding it a light- brown face, a small dark brown nose. Pointed ears stood at the end, with a light peach and pink complexion on the inside.

The reflection staring back at me from the water was unfamiliar, yet oddly comforting. My light brown antlers, though not as grand as the first deer I had seen, but quite impressive. All this time, I had known I was a deer, but seeing my face in the water for the first time stirred something within me. There, in that moment, I felt the weight of realization—this was who I truly was. The awareness hit me like a wave, and for a moment, I lost myself.

The others had already started drinking. The water level was very low, and I had to wade in deeper to reach it. As I dipped my legs into the pond, a surprising warmth spread through me. There wasn't much time to think – the herd was gulping down the water as fast as they could. I bent my neck and licked the surface, hoping to quench my thirst, but barely any water made its way into my mouth. The others seemed to be drinking at a ravenous pace, and panic began to creep in. I wasn't about to be left behind again.

Without thinking, I closed my eyes and plunged my face into the water, licking and gulping as quickly as I could. I was frantic, almost desperate, but finally, I was able to drink properly. After several minutes, my stomach felt full, and I backed away from the pond. The pond was nearly empty now. A few others continued drinking until they were satisfied, but most had stopped.

As I stepped onto the soft, green grass, I felt a cooling sensation. I bent down to inspect it, realizing I would soon have to eat this grass—but how? The thought of chewing it seemed far worse than drinking water. The others had already started eating, chomping down at a steady, relaxed pace. I hesitated, then braced myself, lowering my head to take my first bite.

The taste was awful. I had no choice, though, so I began to chew, forcing myself to swallow each bite. My face twisted in disgust with every mouthful, and I could feel the others watching me, some even amused by my struggle. It wasn't that the grass had a strong taste, but its texture reminded me of chewing crumpled paper. Still, I kept going, gulping down as much as I could manage. Eventually, I had eaten enough, though the experience left me unsettled.

I remembered the time I used to eat junk food without giving a single thought. I was so ungrateful.

As the sky darkened, we settled in for the night. The elders stood guard, their watchful eyes scanning the horizon, while the rest of us lay low beneath the stars. I closed my eyes, trying to block out the uneasy feeling and drifted into sleep, right there in the heart of the forest.

The sun's rays coaxed me awake. Around me, the others were already up, grazing on what little grass remained. Soon, we moved on. The water had dried up, and the green patches were nearly gone. As we walked, the sun climbed higher, and I began to feel thirsty again. The ones at the front started making noises, and suddenly, they bolted forward. I didn't know what had excited them, but I found myself running too, and with every step, I realized how natural it felt – my legs moved in perfect harmony, the earth steady beneath me.

Then, after a stretch of running, the sight before us took my breath away.

Everywhere I looked, the landscape was a vibrant sea of green—luscious trees and thick bushes scattered across a juicy carpet of grass that seemed to stretch on forever. The towering trees stood tall and proud, their leafy branches forming a natural canopy, casting dappled shadows that danced on the ground. The cool breeze that rustled through the leaves was a welcome relief from the sun's warmth, like nature's own air conditioning. It felt like stepping into a painting, each stroke of green perfectly placed to create a serene, beautiful scene.

They seemed happy with this place, yet a few of them; to my despair, looked concerned. All of them went to explore the entire place. What a sight it was! There was a magnificent pond, with crystal clear water. My friend and I hopped right over to the edge and began to drink from it. Oh! It felt so soothing to my burning throat. All of a sudden, I felt completely refreshed. I stepped out from there and just kept looking around. I looked at a distance and could see a couple of the baby deer just playing around each other as they roamed around the entire place. Suddenly, a loud grunt came from the other side, from one of the deer.

Hearing that, my friend suddenly got up and stood upright as it became extremely still and quiet. The other children had also stopped with their shenanigans and were now listening. No one uttered a single word as we stood there in silence. I, too, tried my level best and then we could hear it again, the same grunting noise – kind of like a call from over there. All of a sudden, the deer's tail began twitching continuously. I had a feeling that something was wrong.

He looked at me with urgency in his eyes, then turned and began walking back towards where we had come from. Without hesitation, I followed, along with two others. As we reached the entrance, the entire herd was already there—silent, upright, and on edge. Not a single sound was made. Then, the call came one last time, and in an instant, everyone turned and took off in the opposite direction. The whole herd bolted.

I was frozen in confusion until the sound hit me—a roar so ferocious it made every hair on my body stand on end.

Oh no, no, no, no, no…

I glanced back, the roar growing louder with each passing second. Panic surged through me as the herd surged past. I didn't wait for another signal. Without thinking, I turned and ran for my life. My legs, driven by sheer instinct, moved faster than they ever had before. The ground flew by beneath me—rocks, grass, dirt, repeating in a blur. I could hear the pounding hooves of the other deer behind me, but I didn't dare turn back. I didn't want to see what was gaining on us.

"Run... you crazy boy-slash-deer. Run for your life, or this'll be the shortest of all your lives. Run!" I said to myself.

I bolted towards a dense cluster of trees, hoping to conceal myself in their cover. But as I weaved through the forest, dodging thick branches and jagged rocks, I realized I was completely alone. The herd had vanished. All I could hear were fast-paced footsteps echoing around me. My heart pounded in my chest, and pain shot through my feet as I stepped on sharp rocks. But I couldn't stop now, not when danger was so close behind.

Suddenly, I glanced back—and that was my mistake. I didn't see the massive tree directly in front of me. Before I could react, I slammed into it with full force.

The impact knocked the wind out of me, and I tumbled to the ground. My entire body ached, my head throbbed, and the world spun around me. I struggled to sit up, but everything hurt. Through the dizziness, I heard the fast footsteps of the other deer fading away. Panic set in as I realized I was alone.

But then, to my relief, one of the deer who had taken the same route as me approached, his slowed footsteps crunching softly on the ground. He nudged me gently, helping me get back on my feet. I staggered up, grateful for the help, and together we pushed forward into the dense woods.

The forest was dark, the ground beneath us damp and sticky. Thick tree canopies blocked out the sunlight, casting everything in shadow. The air was heavy, and the sounds of the herd had disappeared entirely. We moved cautiously, unsure of where to go or what lay ahead for us.

I cannot believe my one wrong decision led to this. Being

a human was so easy, yet, I took it all for granted and now I was trapped in this deranged hellhole.

We needed water, shelter, anything that could offer us safety. But for the first time, I realized something far more unsettling: surviving here wasn't just about finding food or water. We were prey. And as that truth sank in, I was hit with the terrifying reality of this life—every day would be a fight for survival, a relentless race to stay alive.

This wasn't just one close call. It was one of many. I would have to spend my whole life running, just to live... to live my life.

The entire area was engulfed in pitch blackness, and a shiver ran down my spine. The shadows closed in around me, making it difficult to navigate as I stumbled over sudden dips, rocks, and rolling pebbles beneath my hooves. In that moment, I was transported back to one of my scariest memories—a class field trip from the previous year or my previous human life. Almost everyone in my class had gone, and my fondness for animals led me to believe I'd have a great time. It was a day trip, and we'd packed sandwiches for the journey. We spotted a few deer, some antelope, and even a couple of monkeys in the forest. Everything had gone surprisingly well until we stopped for a bathroom break during the jeep ride. When I returned, I was met with sheer panic: both jeeps had left without me.

That was the scariest moment of my life. I remember feeling like I was destined to become someone's lunch that day. Hiding beneath a large tree, I felt utterly alone, just as I did now. The silence was deafening, and my heart raced as if it might burst from my chest. Familiar waves of fear and anxiety washed over me, rendering me paralyzed, frozen in place.

The sharp prickly thorns and sudden patches of weeds sprouting from the ground added to my unease. Suddenly, I heard a loud snap behind me. I whipped around, heart pounding, only to find my companion stepping on a twig. Relief flooded through me, but the eerie atmosphere still gripped my heart. It felt like an unseen predator was lurking nearby, and I was completely in the dark about it.

Worse yet, I had no one to rely on. True, I had one other deer with me, but he felt more like a liability than a support. I scanned the area, desperate for a safe place to rest. After what felt like hours of stumbling through the darkness, I finally spotted a more secure spot, nestled between two towering trees, offering some protection from the front and back. A massive rock anchored the left side, leaving only the right side exposed.

This seemed like a decent enough hideaway. Both of us were exhausted, and the moment we settled down, my eyelids grew heavy. Within moments, I drifted off into the land of dreams.

When I awoke, the sunlight filtered through the trees, and I felt a wave of relief wash over me. The world was much less frightening in the light of day. The leaves rustled in the gentle breeze, and the damp grass beneath me resembled a handwoven coffee table rug, inviting and soft.

Though the sun blazed overhead, the towering trees created a natural canopy that shielded us from its harsh rays, providing a perfect, cool refuge. As I looked around, I noticed the other deer nearby, standing on his hind legs and plucking leaves from lower branches. It was a funny sight—he was creating a surprisingly stable balance, tiptoeing on his hind feet while munching with enthusiasm. In that moment, the fear of the night melted away, replaced by a sense of wonder at the simplicity of nature and the joy of companionship.

I approached him and attempted the same trick, but instead of pulling leaves, I fell straight to the ground. Seeing me tumble, he burst into a smile, his tail wagging with delight. I couldn't help but laugh back at his infectious joy. I tried a few more times, and with one last attempt, I found the perfect stance. Leaning forward, I reached for the leaves and munched down. It wasn't the tastiest, but it was satisfying enough.

Once again, I rose to my hind legs, nibbling and tugging at the greenery. After a while, both of us were full and content. We sprawled out, basking in this momentary peace, not knowing when we might next be forced to flee for our lives. This spot felt perfect for resting. Reluctantly, we knew we would have to leave and keep moving on. It would be best if we could reunite with the herd—just the two of us would stand no chance against a predator.

As we looked ahead, the next stretch revealed an uphill climb with trees and grass forming a steep slope that seemed to stretch on for miles. I glanced at him; he returned my gaze and nodded in that direction. We were ready to set off again. Let the games begin.

This time, both of us felt less anxious. In fact, we were slightly more relaxed—watchful, but at ease. We continued our ascent, the terrain becoming steeper with each step. Our throats began to dry, urging us to seek water. Just when hope seemed dim, fortune smiled upon us—a shimmering stream glimmered in the distance, just off the main path.

We sprinted towards it, and what a sight it was! The lush

green trees surrounded the stream, the water flowing gently, inviting us to quench our thirst. We bent down and drank deeply, relief washing over us. This was perfection. Everything seemed to align for our day—pleasant weather, a temperate breeze that neither burned nor chilled us, just the right comfort.

After satisfying our thirst, frolicked by the stream, and attempted to climb the sturdy branches of the mighty trees but I can verify this fact after experience – deer can in no possible way, climb trees. Time slipped away, and before we knew it, the sun began to dip below the horizon, ushering in the evening. As darkness approached, we knew it was time to be vigilant. While my companion decided to rest, I chose to stay alert. However, fatigue soon overcame me, and before long, my eyes fluttered shut, dragging me into a deep sleep.

Morning came, and for the first time amid this chaos, I felt a sense of tranquillity as I watched him drinking from the stream. Stretching my legs, I savoured the feeling of being well-rested. Turning around, I gazed into the vibrant landscape, feeling like this place was finally mine.

The beautifully sculpted layout revealed trees flowing gracefully, thick roots sprawling beneath a lush canopy. In the distance, a group of monkeys swung effortlessly among the branches, their playful antics captivating my attention. I followed their movements, entranced, when suddenly they halted, all facing a particular direction. Curiosity pulled my gaze upward, and to my horror, I spotted a long, brown gun trained directly at me.

A large black jeep loomed nearby, two men inside, one gripping a gun tightly. Before I could fully grasp the situation or what might happen next, I ducked behind a tree. A loud bang shattered the silence, and I instinctively checked myself for injuries. Suddenly, a wailing cry pierced the air—near the stream! Panic surged through me, and before I could move, another gunshot echoed, amplifying the cry.

***

I was shaken as I closed the book shut. As much as I wanted to continue reading, I had to complete some pending work. I dove into research for some great designs and paint shades for my project, excitement bubbling up as I gathered ideas. By the time I wrapped everything up, it was nearly lunchtime. The meal was ready; it just needed reheating.

"Hey, I'm planning to eat my sandwich right now. Should I warm one up for you right now?" I asked Jason as I headed outside the room.

"No, no. You go ahead. I just ordered a pizza and it'll be arriving in about ten minutes," he replied.

I went inside the kitchen and turned on the light. I was looking for something that would pair well with my sandwich. I finally settled on a small packet of chips and a lemonade. I turned off the lights as I headed back to my room. I started munching on my sandwich as I flipped open the pages and continued to read…

I could hear the tires rolling closer; they were coming. A million thoughts raced through my mind. What could I do? I had no means of defending myself. My knees felt weak, and tears streamed down my cheeks as shivers coursed through me.

I wanted to check on him, to help, but they were relentless. I closed my eyes, a single thought consuming me, and then I took off, feeling their gaze upon me as I fled.

Gunshots rang out, whizzing past me, and I dove deeper into the forest. I hoped they had lost me. Just like that, I was alone again—waiting to be hunted, to be torn apart by some predator or shot by hunters. I collapsed on the forest floor, the image of the other deer flashing in my mind. I couldn't believe what had just transpired. Just like that, he was gone. All this struggle for survival, and what kind of life was this? Running—always running to live—that was all it had ever been, and it felt like it always would be. No freedom. No escape from this prison.

I trudged through the endless maze of trees, the valleys and open spaces visible in the distance, yet this tangled wilderness offered the best chance for survival. I wandered from one hiding spot to another, feeling nauseous, until I sank down behind a large tree. In front of me stood a cluster of thorny shrubs with only one exit. All around me was the relentless buzzing of insects. I felt so weak that when I tried to stand, my body refused to cooperate. I was trapped in a bubble that wouldn't break. Before long, my eyes shut tight, and I drifted off to sleep. It felt like only a few hours had passed, but now the temperature was unbearable.

Despite the canopy offering shade, I could feel the stifling heat around me. My throat was parched, and the oppressive air was suffocating. Gunshots echoed in my mind, replaying again and again. The face of that deer haunted me, and I burst into tears. Just like that, he was gone. All the fighting, all the running, all the blood, sweat, and tears seemed like a futile existence.

Earlier, I had worried about a simple paper—a questionnaire that had made me cry over how hard I had worked for it. In retrospect, that seemed nothing compared to this. I doubted I could survive much longer. I wandered aimlessly, feeling like a lost spirit. I forced myself to eat a few bites of grass, just enough to sustain me for another day.

Looking around, I found nothing—no sounds, no footsteps of other deer, no roars of tigers, no screeching tires—just an eerie silence. I summoned the courage to search for water; my throat felt like sandpaper. After hours on the prickly trail, I finally stumbled upon a tiny pond. It was nothing like the earlier one, but it would suffice for now.

As the temperature dropped and the sun began to set, I found a cozy spot to rest. I stood in the pond, gazing at my reflection. My beady black eyes, brown snout, tiny circular ears, and rustic antlers stared back at me. What kind of trick had fate played? How had I transformed from a young boy into this creature? It felt surreal, a reflection that seemed like a lie. After taking a few last sips of water, I settled down behind a mighty tree, exhaustion overtaking me once more. Before I knew it, I was out cold again.

The next morning, my eyes fluttered open, one at a time. I stretched my legs slowly, feeling the stiffness ease as I stood up. Reassuring myself that everything would be alright—that I would reunite with the others soon—I decided it was time to venture into the open. Just as I began to step out, a rustle behind me caught my attention. I turned to look, but found nothing. Still, an unsettling feeling gripped me. It was as if my instincts were warning me; deer have an uncanny ability to sense danger, and I had finally learned to trust that intuition.

I stood perfectly still, like a statue, ears straining for the slightest sound. Just as I was about to step out for a drink from the pond, a flash of movement caught my eye. Panic surged through me—I saw the reflection of a fierce paw, orange and white with black stripes. As the leg lifted, the unmistakable face of the predator came into view. The orange visage with white markings and piercing black stripes glared at me, embodying raw, predatory ferocity. My heart raced, pounding like a drum, and I froze, paralyzed by fear. One step forward, and I'd be torn to shreds. One step back, and I'd still be trapped. I closed my eyes, counting in my head: "3… 2… 1…" and then I bolted in the opposite direction, my legs kicking off the ground like never before. The beast was right on my tail.

I dove into the underbrush, zigzagging between trees, leaping over roots and rocks, my body stumbling but refusing to stop. I felt the earth shift beneath me—soil, water, and debris flying with each frantic stride. I couldn't look back; one wasted second could mean my end. Just then, a loud gunshot shattered the air, and I felt a sharp pain pierce my leg. I crashed to the ground, hitting the earth hard.

The pain was unbearable, a torment I had never known before. I wanted to die right there, beneath the serene sky, where clouds drifted lazily and the sun shone bright. But then another bang echoed, and a bullet struck my stomach. Blood spilled from the wound, warmth flooding my body as pain shot through me like fire. I was seized by agony, my body uncontrollable. Tears streamed from my eyes as the landscape around me began to swirl—sky, trees, clouds merging into a chaotic whirlpool.

And then, just like that, everything faded into a dark abyss of nothingness.

That was it for today. I couldn't go on. I felt sadness as I read through that section. The image of the poor little deer lying in the mud, begging for freedom yet unable to escape, nearly brought me to tears.

Feeling sleepy, I wondered if I had fully caught up on rest. I carefully tucked the stack of sheets back into my nightstand and dozed off.

CHAPTER 9

TWO FINS AND A TALE

A couple of hours later, I was stirred awake by my mom, gently shaking me.

"Get up, Belle! Don't you have practice? Hurry, I've made oatmeal for you. Eat, get dressed, and let's go!" I glanced at the clock, still half-asleep—it was just past six. Panic surged through me. I quickly got dressed, 'inhaled' my oatmeal and rushed out with mom for practice.

The routine was almost complete; we just needed to refine our performance. School was a total bust today. There were the most boring lectures of all – history, geography etc. Plus, I was extremely tired. I swear, if I was sitting on the last bench, I would have dozed off. I kept yawning throughout the day. The recital was next Saturday, exactly a week away, and each session left me utterly drained. Today's practice had been especially exhausting.

By the time I got home, I finished my dinner and collapsed onto my bed.

The next morning, I woke up early and decided to go for a run. I met a few friends from my building, but I still felt a bit bored. Susan and Camille usually dropped by on weekends, or we would meet up somewhere to play cards or watch a movie together. It felt odd without them around—they still weren't ready to move on.

Later, the four of us had lunch together, and afterward, Mom and Dad retreated to their room for a nap. Jason lounged on the couch, absorbed in the television.

"Hey, do you want to do something. Perhaps a game of cards or something. I'll let you win this time," I mocked him. However, his eyes stayed glued to the television. I tried snapping my fingers to get his attention.

"Not now Belle. I'm damn tired. Maybe some other time," he replied. I looked back at him in annoyance. I would forget that he could be so useless sometimes.

I went back to my room, quietly opened my book, and continued reading.

***

After what felt like an eternity, my eyes slowly fluttered open, and my head spun uncontrollably. As I glanced around, everything appeared overwhelmingly gigantic once more. Suddenly, a small wave of water splashed across my face, and it took a moment to register—I was completely submerged, floating in water. To my surprise, I could see clearly underwater. My entire body felt strange, rigid, as if a rod had been inserted, forcing me into a streamlined position.

When I tried to move my hands, horror struck me; I saw two orangish fins flapping around. Turning in disbelief, I encountered a sight that shocked me to my core—a goldfish! With its black button-like eyes and slimy, scaly skin shimmering in the light, it was flopping about in the water. I was staring into a mirror and looking at a GOLDFISH! A scream caught in my throat escaped only as a series of bubbles in the water. My splashy tail danced rhythmically in the current, but my stomach churned with nausea.

What on earth was happening?

As I took in my surroundings, the distorted view of the room curving around me became undeniable. I realized I was trapped in a typical round fishbowl, with an opening at the top for air. Oh my God! I was Sparky—the pet fish of my childhood best friend, Max! I used to visit Max almost every day, and Sparky was a constant presence in his home. I marvelled at the little fish, often spending hours watching him swim, pretending to create earthquakes by shaking the bowl and laughing as I poked at him playfully. Those were such joyful times that I longed to relive, memories that warmed me but also made me miss Max dearly. If only his father hadn't transferred jobs; he might still be living just two blocks away.

"Wow, a goldfish—this is definitely a new twist," I thought, bemused. Just when I thought my situation couldn't get any weirder, here I was, a pet goldfish.

My reverie was abruptly interrupted by a loud noise echoing from the hall. I floated across the bowl, quickly realizing my entire world was confined to its small circumference. Turning around, I gasped as a massive human face loomed over me, peering through the glass. It looked like a monster, perhaps even a terrifying one. Suddenly, the bowl jolted violently, as if an earthquake had struck.

Loud snorts and laughter erupted as the world shook around me. Just then, two enormous faces pressed against the glass, their massive foreheads and unsettling eyes sending a jolt of fear through me. In a panic, I tried to escape, swirling through the water at maximum speed, hoping to frighten them away.

To my dismay, it didn't work; their eyes remained glued to the glass. Resigning myself, I decided to wait them out, which was difficult under the intense scrutiny that felt like stage lights shining directly on me. Thankfully, after a few tense moments, they lost interest and moved away, their giant heads retreating as they grabbed their backpacks. One of them appeared shorter and smaller than the other, a fleeting detail lost in my chaotic thoughts.

Feeding Sparky—of course, it made sense. I recognized the blue fish food packet; it must be a common staple for pet fish everywhere. I gazed at the blobs of food floating on the surface, but I didn't feel inclined to try it. Right now, I was completely full. Maybe later, when hunger struck, I'd have to eat it. Let it float for a while, I thought.

After what felt like hours, I sensed the boys returning from school. The door creaked open, and one of them entered. No way! I could vaguely make out the face of the younger, smaller one, and disbelief washed over me. As the door shut, my suspicions were confirmed. There he was, the familiar face, the same curly black hair, with the earlier moustache now morphed into a full beard.

I was looking at my friend—my old friend—who seemed much bigger now after what must have been three or four years. Suddenly, everything clicked into place. Even though the place felt completely new, with unfamiliar furniture and an altered atmosphere, it still held the essence of our childhood.

I felt overjoyed to see him. The smaller one was Max; the three of us had shared so many good times together. I wanted to run up to him and punch him playfully for moving so far away.

The door slammed shut as both boys plopped down, their clothes crumpled as if they had wrestled their way home—which, knowing them, was likely the case. Their mother appeared and handed them some juice, which they drank eagerly before retreating to their rooms. I sat there, trying to absorb everything that had transpired in the last few hours, and especially in those fleeting minutes. It was all too much for me.

I remained dazed for the rest of the day, a million thoughts racing through my head. What cruel prank was God playing on me? Eventually, hunger began to gnaw at me; being submerged in water had drained my energy, and I knew it was time to eat.

I just hoped the food wouldn't be the kind that made me want to puke it back up immediately. Eyeing the floating food particles, I approached one, opened my mouth, and took a cautious nibble. Oh God! It tasted like a rubber ball—extremely salty. I quickly swam away, splashing water at it in an attempt to move it aside.

I glanced at the remaining chunks, disheartened. When would this day end? I peered through the glass bowl. Sometime later, their dad returned from work, sinking into the sofa while the whole family chatted away about their day.

I remembered the times at home when Dad would usually be back for dinner. And that was the common time that the three of us would get together and talk to each other and ask about each one's day. Lately, the three of us hadn't had a meal in a long time. Dad would usually be late from work and even on the days he would come early, I, like an idiot would take my plate inside to watch in front of the television. He never said anything about it but I shouldn't have been like that. Oh, what I would give to go back to those times and if I had a second chance, I would have spent the maximum time with my parents.

I was brought back to the place with all the commotion going on in the living room.

The two boys fired up the PlayStation, controllers in hand, instantly engrossed in their game. Their father went to freshen up, and their mother returned to the kitchen. I spent the next few hours attempting to catch glimpses of the TV screen, desperate for any source of entertainment. Soon enough, they shut down the game, and the entire family gathered around the dining table, just a couple of feet away from me.

I watched them, chatting about the most random topics, passing around clean white plates adorned with floral designs, and spreading an array of mouth-watering dishes across the table. The clatter of cutlery and the sound of food being plopped onto plates created a continuous backdrop of camaraderie and laughter. Inside, I felt a deep pang of longing.

Seeing them together reminded me of my own family once again, and the sight made me miss mine so painfully. It gnawed at me, an ache that felt like it was consuming me. One foolish decision had led me to this endless cycle of regret.

"So, how did your day go, boys?" Mr. Jefferson asked.

"Oh, the usual," they replied in unison. "School was a bit boring, but football practice was awesome! This one here got kicked in the nuts and was on the floor for a good

twenty minutes!" Max exclaimed, pointing at his brother and bursting into laughter, barely able to finish his sentence.

"Ahh," their father replied, clearly unfazed, as this was not new territory for him.

After a while, everyone had eaten to their heart's content, and the table was cleared. I stayed glued to one side of the bowl, my eyes fixated on the scene before me. After what felt like a gruelling day, the lights dimmed, and I tried to relax, closing my eyes and resting at the bottom, but sleep eluded me. It was agonizingly difficult to drift off without a physical body to lie down.

After what felt like an eternity, I finally managed to fall asleep. It couldn't have been more than half an hour, but God only knew how long it actually was when the lights snapped back on.

Oh no! I could hear the noises from all over the house—footsteps echoing, the boys getting shouted at, their dad rushing about, and their mom hurrying up and down the hall. It was complete chaos. The ground shook beneath me as two faces loomed on either side of the bowl. And just like that, they vanished. Their dad came rushing out, plopped down at the kitchen table, inhaled his food, and dashed out the door.

"Drive safely!" shouted Mrs. Jefferson from the kitchen, too busy to check on anyone, happy just to know they were all off to their respective tasks.

She continued her work, arranging the space and hauling a mountain of clothes to fold. A delicious aroma wafted through the air, hinting at another tasty meal being prepared. But just as that thought crossed my mind, more food was plopped into the bowl from above. Oh no! I had barely managed to eat one bite, and now there was so much more.

I hadn't eaten in the last 24 hours, and my stomach made gurgling noises. I looked at the pieces floating around me and decided I had to empty the bowl; this hunger was unbearable.

What followed was a gruesome and unpleasant experience. I won't get into the specifics, but let's just say it left me with a queasy aftertaste that could lead to a vomit explosion at any moment. I managed to keep it down, but I felt bloated, struggling to stay upright as my belly expanded.

Exhausted from the night before and deprived of sleep, I slipped into my resting zone. The light filtering through the windows made it difficult to relax, but soon I felt too comfortable to care. After a couple of hours, I woke to the sound of talking and the television blaring. Everyone was back home, and it seemed to be late at night. I looked outside; it was pitch dark.

Uh oh! My stomach rumbled, letting out gas, bubbles rising to the top. Oh no! It felt like my stomach was tightening by the second. I couldn't hold it in any longer, and before I had time to react, my body clamped down, and poop squirted out into the water.

Eww! It floated beside me, swirling slowly and drifting from one end of the bowl to the other. I looked outside; they were all comfortably settled on their cozy sofas, while I was stuck here, my own poop occupying the same space as me, spreading and contaminating my surroundings with every passing moment. The night stretched out ahead of me, feeling even longer than the previous one, and the thought of my own waste brushing against my face kept me wide awake.

Ewww. I could imagine small pieces of poop just floating

around. Yuck, made me want to puke. One of our neighbours had a goldfish and I remember seeing little round balls of their shit just floating in the tank. Mr. and Mrs. Swift got so fed up with cleaning the tank that, after their pair of fish died, they simply removed the entire thing.

I got out of bed as I had to use the washroom urgently, but I was just waiting for the chapter to end. I brushed my teeth and once again, curled back into bed. I continued on with the book.

CHAPTER 10

EMPTY GLASS BOWL

After what felt like an endless stretch of mind-numbing torture, the next day finally arrived. By now, I was accustomed to the usual morning chaos: the yelling, the scrambling to get up, footsteps echoing everywhere, and the earthquake of movement around me. (Oh God! I really thought I was going to end up eating my own poop. I have no idea how I escaped that fate.)

The family gobbled down breakfast and raced toward the door, leaving a whirlwind of activity in their wake.

Next came the cooking and cleaning, and just as Mrs. Jefferson was about to add more revolting food bits into the tank, she noticed the dirt forming at the edges and the giant piece of pudding my body had left behind. Thank my lucky stars! She picked up the fish tank and carried me, which I assumed was to the kitchen.

As I was taken across the hall, I realized why she spent so much time in this lively space. The kitchen was a warm blend of light brown and yellow, perfectly complemented by a walk-in pantry, cutting-edge blenders, and a giant beige refrigerator. I saw spices neatly arranged in little cubicles, another row of water bottles, and a yellow chopping board adorned with a colorful assortment of vegetables.

Mrs. Jefferson set me down at the sink. I felt a bit nervous; I should have been happy that the entire place was about to get cleaned. Instead, thoughts of what could happen filled my mind. What if I fell straight into the dustbin below? What if I died from being out of water for too long? I started to zigzag aimlessly, my anxiety growing.

While I was lost in my thoughts, the lid of my glass bowl was lifted, revealing the off-white ceiling and a giant hand hovering above. Before I could react, the bowl was lifted, and I was pulled into the air, water splashing all around me as I fell headfirst into a shallow, circular vessel. Was this going to be my new home, or was it just a temporary stay?

I could easily jump out, but what would I do in the open? Probably die in ten seconds. So, I zigzagged from one end to the other. After about 10-15 minutes, I felt the vessel being lifted again, and I was swirled through the current before creating a big splash as I was thrown back into my original bowl. It looked so much better; the water was clearer, and the glass was shiny.

I returned to my usual spot, thinking, "Well, that was a wild experience." After that, the day unfolded much like before: the same evening routine, the same family members bustling about—talking, running, playing, and chattering throughout the house. Even though I knew them all so well, I couldn't help but envy the bond they shared. All I could do was watch from my empty glass bowl.

As the daytime lights flickered on, the familiar scramble of footsteps echoed through the house. The boys startled me with their usual antics, a surprise that was less frightening with each passing day. They quickly gobbled down their food and vanished from the house. Then came the big man, performing the same hurried ritual of eating and shoe-tying before heading out the door.

"You guys could just wake up ten minutes earlier and actually enjoy the delicious meals that Aunty prepared for you! But no, everything is taken for granted, just like I did," I thought, feeling embarrassed as I watched them. I realized I was even worse; I would clunk a portion of available food into my hand and make my own hurried exit. I never thanked my mom for always putting breakfast on the table and instead disrespected her by behaving this way.

Meanwhile, the rest of the kitchen buzzed with activity. Mrs. Jefferson roamed the house, cleaning, washing, and drying. I, on the other hand, barely finished my sleep and managed to swallow a few gooey paper balls—such was my day.

Later that evening, the commotion increased, the chatter filled the air, and excitement seemed to ripple through the household. I couldn't understand why or catch on to what they were discussing, but something felt different. That night, as I fell asleep, it was much easier to rest after learning the techniques of the day. But let me tell you, even sleeping here was a pain in the ass.

It was so hard to find rest when I had nothing to lie on. I had never experienced a "deep sleep" state; all my attempts felt like mere snaps of rest, constantly interrupted. Before I knew it, it was the next day.

For some reason, today was even more chaotic than usual. Everyone seemed to be awake at the same time, and the murmurs filled the air. Strangely, no light was coming from the kitchen. As I looked around, I suddenly saw all the family members emerging at once, stylishly dressed—the boys in matching black jackets, the father in a simple polo shirt and shades, and the mother wearing a brand-new yellow pastel top with comfy tracks and a matching jacket. Her hair and makeup were perfectly done. This family was truly something else. To top it all off, they were lugging around enormous suitcases. Ohhh, so that was what last night had been about!

They had planned a trip, and judging by the size of the suitcases, it seemed like a long one. Last-minute items were being tossed into bags, doors were being locked, and I could hear yelling from the bathroom. Windows were being shut, discussions rushed, and suddenly, they were all rushing out.

"Wait, take me along with you! I don't want to be floating around here in this state of nothingness. Take me with you!" I thought desperately. Of course, I couldn't voice these thoughts; they remained trapped within me.

Before I knew it, they were all out the door, and I heard the loud clicks of the locks from outside. "Of course, of course, robbers and safety and all." I looked around the tank, taking in the crystal-clear water. A sinking realization struck me. In all this commotion, she hadn't dumped any of those ridiculous yet life-saving gooey balls into the tank. Nor was this tank going to be cleaned for who knew how many days. Uh oh! Things were not looking good.

The rest of the day dragged on, me staring out of the bowl, longing for someone to rescue me from this prison of boredom. I spent hours flopping around in the tank, swimming aimlessly. The day passed slowly; I was utterly bored, with nothing else to occupy my mind. I took what little rest I could, sitting in a dull stupor.

The next day dawned—or at least it felt like it. I could gauge the time by staring out the window, observing the light and its colors as dictated by Mother Nature. That was my only guide. All the lights were off, leaving me with little to do. It got dark quickly.

After a few hours of bright sunlight, it would become swelteringly hot outside—well, not for me, living in my aquatic bowl—but the rays became harsh. I guessed it was around noon by then. A couple of hours later, and bam! It would plunge into pitch darkness.

When I heard slight chatter from outside, I knew it was around 9 or 10 PM, and when howling echoed through the night, I recognized it was the middle of the night. That marked the last time I tried to follow the conventional rhythm of life. After that, it was just a giant mess. I slept whenever, woke whenever—there was nothing for me to do. So, I often lay flat on the glass floor or clung to the side of the bowl, yearning to go outside and do something meaningful with my time.

The irony was cruel. All this while, I wanted to while away my time when I was a human. I would just wish that I could just while away my time and now, after my 'wish' had been granted, I couldn't cope with the fact that I had nothing to do. I was a complete mess.

One day, I swam up to the surface and raised my face above the water. Ah! Finally, some dryness, finally something that wasn't wet—something normal. But just a few seconds later, instinct pulled me back down into the water. I wanted to see how long I could survive out of it.

I swam to the surface and stuck my head out, counting the seconds. Not going to lie, it felt pretty normal, albeit a little weird—good weird. After what felt like a few minutes, I started to tire. Staying in that position was difficult, so I decided to dive back down. I could have easily lasted another half hour. Yup, that was another day of mine—might I say, a very productive one.

At this point, I was filled with regret. When I was living my normal life, I had all the time in the world—time to do everything I wanted. I could explore every corner of the house, study as much as I wanted, and excel in my work. I could solve a thousand math problems over and over again—anything but this.

I would have given my parents a big hug, thanking them for everything. I would have hung out with my friends, sharing stories and creating memories. I wanted to learn an instrument, master a dozen languages, try out new dance styles—the list went on and on. I had my whole life in front of me, and I wasted it all away. I let it slip through my fingers. So what if I failed one stupid test? That was nothing compared to the opportunities I had to let go. I wanted everything to go back to the way it was—just the old days. If I could, I would seize every chance and strive for more than just a successful career.

I hated this time with all my heart. I would trade any of my other adventures for this one. Sure, I was safe from predators and harm, but I was cut off from the world, not knowing when this would end. Not to mention, I was feeling extremely hungry.

At this point, if there were another fish in this bowl, it wouldn't have survived. It had been days since I last ate my disgusting food. I was living in the same water, surrounded by the by-products of my body—the piss mixed in, creating a horrible stench I couldn't escape. And then there was the poop, swirling around and settling at the bottom. So much for lying around on the floor.

A few days passed...

In the beginning, I floated aimlessly in this giant bathtub. Even as a kid, I loved to swim and was pretty good at it. I thought this was it—no homework, no annoying people, no studying—just me and this vast pool of water. But now, this endless floating was starting to get on my nerves. I was agitated, and even though I was a lazy guy, I wanted to do something—anything to make my brain think, to stop contemplating how I would spend possibly the last bits of my life in utter dullness.

The possibly last bits of my life, and this was how it would be? Me, living for years, waiting for the slow release of death as I descended into madness. What if I had actually gone mad? What if this was a cruel trick played by my mind? What if I was in a mental hospital, trapped in a nightmare, endlessly shifting bodies? Oh no, no, no, no, no!

Just then, the loud cawing of a crow snapped me out of my spiral of madness. And no, not completely—I was still floating around, wagging my gold and orange tail as I drifted from one end of the bowl to the other.

"Oh god! Please, someone, take me out of this. I can't bear it anymore." If I hadn't gone crazy before, I definitely would have lost my mind by now. Who knows what's real and what's not? Certainly not me. I gazed up at the clear white ceiling,

then turned to the mirror behind me. I kept opening and shutting my eyes for a good couple of minutes, not knowing what I was hoping for. Would I suddenly turn back into a human? Would I grow wings and fly out? Instead of seeing these fins and my orangeish appearance, I wanted to see the Michael Jordan poster on the ceiling of my bedroom—the first thing I used to see when I opened my eyes.

Days passed and I was still trapped in this whirlpool of filth. That's all I could see—me, floating in muck. The hunger was overwhelming, and I couldn't take it anymore. I needed something, anything. I tried to calm myself, steadying my thoughts and believing they would return soon. I knew I had no choice but to have faith that I would survive. It was the same situation every single minute, hour, day. The next few days slipped by, and I lost the will to swim. I just stayed in one little corner of the fishbowl, lacking the enthusiasm or strength to move.

I had become so accustomed to the painted picture of the hall and the dining table that even when I closed my eyes, the same image would pop into my head. I opened my eyes, and there it was: the empty sofas, the spotless white tiles, the quiet wind howling against the windowpane. I couldn't take it anymore. I wanted to jump out, run around, play—anything but sit here in this fishbowl, waiting for someone to join me, waiting to witness some incident, something exciting to break this scary monotony of life. I used to think making decisions was frightening, that change was intimidating. But I was wrong. The real terror was doing nothing.

Just observing life from the side lines, leading a quiet, fearful existence in the background of this fast-paced, opportunistic world. In a peculiar way, my life as a boy mirrored my current situation. Back then, I didn't take action—literally, I did nothing. I did the bare minimum to avoid falling behind. But I had already fallen behind: in friendships, in my relationship with family, in my interests, work, hobbies—everything that mattered most and shaped who I was. Worst of all, I had fallen behind with myself.

It was hard to fall asleep when regret consumed my thoughts. There was nothing to do, nothing to look forward to. Yet, through all these experiences, I learned something strange about the mind and soul. No matter the circumstances, no matter the odds, and no matter the outcome, the human mind is wired to survive. The soul will not give up, no matter what, until the very last breath.

As long as the body could respond, it would strive to live. And so would I. I didn't know what stubbornness resided in this body, but I couldn't turn back now. It had almost been two weeks since I last heard anyone speak. I lay flat on the bottom of the tank, unmoving for days. Raising my head felt like a monumental task. Breathing became difficult, and I found myself gasping for air.

My head throbbed painfully. I had no idea what to do. There was little I could do. I guess it was time. My brain didn't seem to function properly anymore. So, I quietly lay on the tank's surface, trying to draw in as much air as possible. I shifted my body towards the windowsill, looking out.

Ah! It was pitch dark outside. The howling was now unmistakable. I closed my eyes, focusing on my breathing, and that was the last time I saw myself in my yellow and orange clothing.

CHAPTER 11

BETRAYAL

I shut the pages, feeling the weight of sadness linger. At least that boy had realized the true value of human life. You know what? I often took my parents for granted, too. I should definitely be more grateful and thank them for the little things they always did. I was determined to pursue big dreams as well. I wasn't quite sure what I wanted to do when I became a proper adult, but I knew it had to be something significant. Wasted potential was one of the saddest things in life, and nothing was worse than living with regrets. That day, I felt more resolved than ever, thankful for everything—until the next day brought a complete shock.

The morning started off fine. I woke up on time for school and enjoyed a delicious breakfast, thanking my mom, which brought a smile to her face. The day unfolded like any other, until the last two classes after lunch: art. When I went to my locker to grab my things, I found it already open. I was sure I had locked it.

To my horror, as I swung the door open, my art project lay drenched in water or some gooey liquid. As I picked up the remnants, a piece crumbled in my hands and fell to the floor. Big red paint marks slashed across my drawing. Tears filled my eyes as I witnessed the tragedy of my ruined artwork. Rage boiled inside me; this was no accident. All my hard work was completely destroyed.

I rushed into class, my artwork clutched tightly in my hands. Just as I entered, the bell rang, and everyone turned to look at me. A few students had no idea what was happening, but a group of girls on the side started laughing and smirking, casting fake pity my way.

I was furious. I imagined beating them up with their own fists. "Good one, guys," one girl sneered at Susan and Camille, who looked guilty. "She deserves it—acting like such a goody-goody and always first in everything," she continued.

I glared at them; they looked abashed.

"Really, you guys?! This was your doing?!" I shouted.

"Wait—we can explain," they said, but I didn't want to hear any of it. I stormed out of the classroom, consumed by rage, and ran to the bathroom.

I was seething. I wanted to punch them, their actions had crossed a line. I didn't want to see their faces again. Eventually, I returned to class because I couldn't hide in the bathroom forever. The teacher asked about my project, and I told her everything. She screamed at the girls and gave them a stern reprimand, but that didn't matter to me.

With a gooey mess for an assignment and a deadline looming in two days, I packed my bag. As soon as the bell rang, I rushed out, still fuming. They tried to stop me, attempting to talk, but I was in no mood. I shoved them out of my way and headed home. I couldn't focus on anything else; all I could think about was how I would prepare an entire project in just one day.

But I had to practice for my dance session. I rehearsed a few steps, and before I knew it, it was time to go. I wished I could have spent the day working on my project, but today was important, and I couldn't miss it. Looking back, I probably should have skipped.

During our routine, two pairs in the center performed a simple 'pas de deux,' and all I had to do was execute a split in mid-air. I wasn't trying to sound cocky; it was simple because I had practiced it for over a week and nailed it every time. When my moment came, I leaped into the air. But for some reason, I landed flat-footed—an absolute disaster. I twisted my left ankle and fell to the floor, clutching my foot in agony.

It hurt like hell, and I lay there for a good two minutes. Friends helped me up, but my ankle throbbed painfully. My dad came to pick me up soon after. They had to continue with practice while I was helped into the car. We went straight to the doctor, who diagnosed a sprain. I would need at least two days to heal, and my performance was day after! Fantastic news!

Returning home, I felt utterly dejected. Despite my dad's best efforts to cheer me up, I couldn't muster a smile. Today had been the crappiest day imaginable. I came home in tears, feeling like everything was falling apart. I had worked so hard for this ballet recital, and now it felt like all my effort would be in vain. I tried to sleep that night, but the pain kept me tossing and turning.

I didn't feel like reading. One of the last things I expected was to have a heartfelt moment with Jason. He walked into my room, saw me crying and the crêpe bandage wrapped around my leg, and forgot everything that had happened earlier. He acted like the big brother I had always seen him as. He consoled me and listened as I vented about school and everything that had gone wrong. As we talked, I felt myself getting sleepy. Before I knew it, I had fallen asleep, feeling him tuck me in and straighten my pillow. I let out a soft smile and drifted into deep sleep.

The next morning, I woke up, and everything hit me all at once. I felt grumpy for the first time in ages. There was no point in going to school today; I had to start my artwork from scratch. Jason brought me breakfast before leaving for school, and I realized that, despite the chaos, I was grateful for the support of my family.

I pulled out the pile of pages that had been sitting untouched on my bedside table, the one that had made me reflect on gratitude and wasted potential just days earlier. After everything that had happened—the wrecked painting, the sprained ankle, the fear of missing out on the recital—my mind was buzzing. It felt like a whirlwind of emotions, from anger and frustration to relief and excitement. I needed a moment of quiet, something to ground me before the big day.

I opened the book and began to read. The words flowed more easily this time, like they were meant to reach me at this exact moment. The characters' struggles with their own challenges mirrored mine in an odd way. They had experienced loss, disappointment, and pain, yet they kept going, just like I had.

A realization settled in as I read: setbacks, no matter how big or small, are temporary. My painting could be replaced, my ankle could heal, and, even if I hadn't been allowed to perform, life would have gone on. But what mattered most was the effort I had put in and the support of the people around me—my mom, Jason, even Susan and Camille, who had come to apologize. I wasn't alone in this journey.

As the words on the page blended into the background, my mind drifted back to the upcoming recital. I imagined the stage, the lights, and the audience clapping after my performance. A sense of peace washed over me. Day after tomorrow, no matter what happens, I know I have already won in a way. I had pushed through, and that was more than enough.

Finally, my eyes grew heavy. I closed the book and placed it back on the table, feeling a quiet confidence settle within me. Day after tomorrow would be a new day—a day where I'd step onto that stage, give it my all, and be proud of everything I had overcome.

With a contented sigh, I drifted off to sleep, ready for whatever came next.

CHAPTER 12

TIME

I leaned over the puddle, expecting to see my own face staring back. What I saw made me recoil. The reflection wasn't human. It was… insect. Slender, segmented, with delicate, veined wings and long, threadlike antennae. My mind struggled to reconcile the image with my own sense of self. Then, a memory surfaced: Ms. Annie's bio lecture, the magnified image of a mayfly projected on the screen. The distinctive markings on the wings… they were the same. I was a mayfly.

But before I could spiral into a full-blown panic, something shifted within me. My wings twitched, and without thinking, I fluttered up into the air again. The panic subsided, replaced by an overwhelming sense of freedom. My human worries—the recital, the misunderstandings with friends, my injury—faded into the background. I was flying. I had no restrictions, no limits. I could explore the world in a way I never could before.

I soared higher, leaving the playground behind. Below me, the city sprawled out in a chaotic mess of noise and movement, but it didn't seem to matter anymore. I was part of something bigger now—part of nature, part of the wind. The mayfly's short life didn't feel so tragic when I was experiencing this. Every second felt amplified, like I was truly alive for the first time.

As I zipped through the air, I saw familiar faces—my friends, my mom, people from my neighborhood—but none of them could see me. I was invisible to them, just another tiny insect buzzing by. It felt strange to be so detached from my human life, yet so connected to the natural world around me.

I drifted back towards the garden, feeling a sense of calm wash over me. Maybe this was what I needed after all—a break from everything, a chance to see the world from a new perspective. I wasn't sure how long I'd stay like this, but for now, I decided to embrace it. I would live every moment like it was my last, just like a mayfly.

At a distance, I could see the swings and a young woman, about thirty or so, pushing a cute baby dressed in white pajamas, grey mittens, and wearing a tiny white cap. It had a special seat, so that the baby could be locked into it. And judging by the look on the baby's face, it was having the time of its life. It let out a few giggles and just hearing that the mother began to laugh. She just couldn't take it anymore.

She unstrapped the baby and just took it into her arms. She looked so happy and just threw the baby gently up into the air, causing it to laugh even more. And then all of a sudden it hit me; I was getting a déjà vu. I had seen this earlier for sure. While looking at the mother's face, I could sense a familiarity but seeing the white cap, the grey mittens and then it hit me, I had seen all of this on that day!

That awful day which lead to everything horrible. I could

recollect the picture as clear as day, I was coming back from school when I walked on this same path that I was on now.

As I pondered on about this thought, every passing second, the same idea kept sinking in. This wasn't just a bizarre adventure anymore—it felt like the story was mirroring my previous life. The mayfly with only 24 hours to live, the young mother and her baby, the familiar sights from that day, the greasy football—everything was leading me towards something. Towards what, though? A second chance?

I couldn't believe I was standing there, staring at the human version of myself from this tiny mayfly form. I watched my human self, sitting on the edge of the bed, tears streaming down my face. What had I been crying about? I couldn't remember, but the sadness felt so palpable, so heavy. It was like I was watching a scene from my life that I had forgotten about, or maybe never understood in the first place. Why had I been so upset?

I fluttered into the room, my tiny wings vibrating with intensity. I knew I didn't have much time. Time was ticking away, and I had no idea what would happen once they were up. But I had to try something. If I was supposed to learn something from this strange journey, it had to be now.

I moved closer to my human self. I hovered in front of my own tear-streaked face, trying to understand what had gone wrong. The pain in my eyes was so raw, like I was carrying the weight of the world on my shoulders. And then it hit me—this was that day. The day I had screwed everything up. The argument, the misunderstanding, the endless spiral of guilt. I remembered now.

The mayfly's short lifespan flashed before me again—just

24 hours to live, and it was all about making the most of it. What had I done with my time back then? Wasted it on things that didn't matter, held onto grudges, let regret consume me. But now… now I had the chance to change that. To do something different. To live differently, even if it was only for these few fleeting moments.

I fluttered closer to my human self, my wings beating faster. I wanted to scream at myself, shake myself out of the misery, tell myself to let it go. But of course, I couldn't. I was just a mayfly, a tiny, insignificant insect with no voice. Or was I?

Without thinking, I landed on my own hand. My human self-flinched at the sensation, looking down at me in confusion. I could see the tears pause for a moment as I crawled up onto my wrist. And in that moment, something strange happened. It was like I could feel a connection—a tiny, fragile link between my mayfly self and my human self.

I couldn't speak, but maybe I didn't need to. Maybe just being there, reminding myself of the fleeting nature of life, was enough. I felt my wings begin to slow, my energy fading. I didn't have much time left.

I looked up at my human self, hoping, praying, that somehow I understood. That somehow, this tiny mayfly could be the sign I needed to let go of the past and move forward. The answer wasn't in the words on the page, but in the feeling that was stirring inside of me.

I darted across the room, trying to stop him from whatever he was about to do. My tiny wings buzzed faster than ever as I flew towards him, desperately trying to get his attention again.

He reached out for something in the drawer, but before

his hand could fully open it, I slammed myself into him once more. This time, I aimed right for his forehead, hoping to shake him out of whatever dark thoughts had returned. He flinched, swatting the air in frustration, but I kept at it. I wasn't going to let him do this.

He groaned in annoyance, but this time he didn't go for the drawer. Instead, he dropped to his bed, lying down with an exhausted sigh. His hand still rested near the handle of the drawer, though, and I could tell that the temptation was still there. I fluttered near his head, watching as his expression slowly softened, the tension in his shoulders easing.

I couldn't help but wonder: what was in that drawer? What had driven him to the edge before? My mind raced with possibilities, but deep down, I knew that it didn't matter what the object was. What mattered was the pain that had led him there in the first place—the same pain I had felt in my human form. And now, I had to stop it.

I perched on the edge of the bed, waiting, watching. He stared at the ceiling, his breathing steadying, the earlier panic and frustration fading. I could sense that my mission wasn't over, but at least for now, I had succeeded in keeping him from doing something irreversible.

Just as I thought the worst had passed, there was a knock on the door. He sat up, wiping his face quickly as his mom entered the room. She didn't say much, just sat beside him on the bed, placing a gentle hand on his back. "Hey, sweetie, everything alright?"

He hesitated, glancing toward the drawer again, but then shook his head, forcing a smile. "Yeah, Mom. Just... tired. It's been a long day."

She gave him a knowing look but didn't press further. Instead, she pulled him into a hug, a silent comfort that seemed to melt the last bit of tension from his body. As she stood to leave, she added, "Don't stay up too late. Get some rest, okay?"

Once she was gone, he lay back down, staring at the ceiling for a long moment. His hand was no longer reaching for the drawer. Instead, it rested beside him, limp and relaxed. He closed his eyes, and I knew the battle had been won—for now.

'Any second now, Dad would enter,' I thought, my tiny wings fluttering anxiously as the giant book slammed into the wall, just missing me by half an inch. My heart raced, and I was sure I wouldn't make it. But then, the door creaked open.

Dad stepped inside, taking in the chaos—his son flustered and teary-eyed, a mess of books and papers strewn across the room. He looked from the scene to his son and simply asked, "How was your paper today?"

That one question was all it took. The poor kid, who had been holding it all in, suddenly burst into tears. He wailed uncontrollably, words spilling out in between sobs. "I don't know what happened, Dad! My brain just... just stopped working! I... I studied so hard, and I still couldn't do it! I failed... I've let you and Mom down."

I hovered nearby, completely still, watching in awe as the boy's emotions flooded the room. It was raw, heart-breaking, and utterly human. He talked about how he'd prepared for weeks, especially for this math test. His nights spent hunched over books, revising, solving problems—his whole life seemed dedicated to this one moment, and it all crumbled.

"I don't get it, Dad," he cried, his voice breaking. "I studied day and night. I... I wanted to make you proud."

Dad stood there, calm and composed, letting his son pour out everything. He didn't interrupt, didn't rush him. And when the boy finally ran out of words, gasping for breath between sobs, Dad took a deep breath and said something that not only stunned the boy but floored me too.

"You know, I've never seen you work this hard before," he began gently, "and no matter what happened in that test today, I'm proud of you for the effort you put in. It wasn't about the grade, son. It was about showing yourself what you're capable of."

He paused, giving the words time to settle in. The boy blinked through his tears, his sobs slowing down as he absorbed the unexpected response.

"This test doesn't define you," Dad continued. "What matters is that you tried your best, and that's more important than any score. So don't beat yourself up. Go easy on yourself. You've earned a break, okay? We'll figure out what comes next together."

The boy stared at his father, tears still glistening in his eyes, but his face had softened. The disappointment was still there, but it was starting to lift. And for the first time in what felt like hours, he smiled—a small, shaky smile, but a smile nonetheless.

"Thanks, Dad," he whispered, his voice hoarse but grateful.

Dad simply smiled back and gave his son a reassuring nod before turning to leave the room. As the door clicked shut behind him, I couldn't help but feel a wave of relief wash over me. For once, everything was going to be alright.

I took one last glance around the room, making sure everything was as calm as it seemed. I fluttered toward the window, finding the same small gap I had squeezed through earlier. As I made my way out into the cool night air, I couldn't help but feel a strange sense of accomplishment. Maybe, just maybe, I had managed to change something this time.

In that moment, I knew. I had broken the cycle. I had found the way out. The mayfly's time was up, but my time… my time was just beginning.

And as I flew off into the vast, endless sky, the stars twinkling above me, I realized that sometimes, it wasn't about fighting fate—it was about being there, in the right moment, to nudge things in a different direction.

As I floated above, soaking in the city's vibrance, the snow gently began to settle on my wings, tiny cold flecks that only added to the serenity of the night. The world below moved as if on a different timeline, completely unaware of the peaceful expanse I was witnessing. It felt like I had transcended the chaos, the worries, and even the pain that had followed me for so long. Up here, everything was just… still.

I kept glancing back at that cozy apartment where the couple was lost in their world. The warmth of their love, their casual intimacy, had filled me with a strange, deep sense of comfort, like watching a movie scene that lingers in your mind long after it's over. Maybe it was the simplicity of it all—a connection that seemed so effortless, like they didn't need anything beyond each other.

But up here, on the rooftop, I had something equally special—solitude. A kind of quiet that allowed me to be fully present in the moment. The distant sounds of the city below—the cars, the faint hum of life—faded as the snow grew heavier, painting the world in a soft white glow. It was as if time had slowed down, letting me breathe for the first time in ages.

The train I had heard earlier passed beneath me, its rhythmic clacking merging with the night. I gazed across the city, tracing the roads with my eyes, each streetlight leading to another unseen story, another world. And though I couldn't see the end of the roads, it didn't matter. The journey itself was enough, for once.

Up here, I was no longer chasing answers or trying to fix what was broken. I wasn't fighting against anything, nor was I trying to change the course of things like before. I simply existed, weightless and content, surrounded by the vastness of the sky and the endless city stretching beneath me. For the first time in what felt like forever, I wasn't thinking about the past, or the future, or what could've been. I was just... here.

The snowflakes began to fall thicker now, covering the rooftops and streets like a fresh canvas, and I found myself smiling—a quiet, genuine smile. There was something beautiful about this moment, something that made me appreciate every breath, every beat of my wings.

Maybe I didn't know what was coming next, but for now, this was enough. The beauty, the stillness, the simple act of watching the world from a distance—it filled me with a sense of peace I hadn't realized I'd been searching for all along.

As I finally looked down, the world seemed so small and yet so intricate, each life a piece of a greater mosaic. I couldn't help but marvel at how everything seemed connected, even if just in passing. I spread my wings wider and let myself glide effortlessly through the cold night air, allowing the wind to carry me wherever it wanted to go.

For now, I was free. And for the first time in a long while, that was enough.

The cold had taken over completely now, biting at my skin, but I refused to move. I was determined to wait it out. The night sky seemed endless, a vast canvas of deep blue and black, dotted with shimmering stars that twinkled like tiny diamonds, some brighter than others. The view was breathtaking. I couldn't remember the last time I'd seen it so clearly, so beautifully.

Snowflakes fell from above, twirling in the wind as it picked up speed. The world around me was wrapped in a silent white blanket, but instead of feeling the chill, I felt warmth—an unfamiliar comfort. I closed my eyes, letting the magic of the moment wash over me. My heart was racing, pounding in my chest, and for once, it wasn't from fear or anxiety—it was from something more profound, something like peace.

As I stood there, eyes shut tight, my mind wandered back to the day that had just passed. It felt like the most important day of my life—the longest and most pivotal. Everything that had led up to this moment, everything that had happened... it was like a slow motion montage playing in my head. The wind howled around me, but inside, there was only calm.

I wished, with all my might, that this was it—a fresh start, a new beginning. I wanted a second chance for him, for me, for all of us. A life where different choices could be made, where the mistakes of the past didn't define the future. Where every possibility felt like an open door, waiting to be walked through.

My hand trembled as I flipped to the next page, desperate to know what would come next, hoping beyond hope that this would be the turning point. I held my breath as the words unfolded before me...

CHAPTER 13

GRATITUDE

After a ray of dizzying lights and a complete blackout, my eyes opened.

Everything was a blur, and by now, I was almost used to the disorientation. As I struggled to focus, a wave of dread swept over me—what could I possibly have turned into this time? Maybe an earthworm, doomed to wriggle across the ground, constantly avoiding someone's shoe. Or worse, a clueless chicken just trying to avoid being turned into someone's dinner.

Yesterday felt like a distant, unreal nightmare. But as my vision cleared, something familiar caught my eye—the Michael Jordan poster, with him mid-dunk, tongue out, wearing that iconic red and white Chicago Bulls jersey!

I blinked. Wait...no, no, this can't be real. My eyes darted around the room. My blue and white cupboards. My PlayStation sitting in front of the TV. My biology textbook lying open on my desk—the test I was supposed to take. No... this can't be happening. I rubbed my eyes furiously, staring at my hands in disbelief.

If this is some twisted dream of being human again while

I'm still stuck as a toad or something, I swear...

I pinched myself. Hard. "Ow!" Okay, that definitely hurt. But pain had never felt so good. I was back—really back.

I shot out of bed and rushed to the mirror. There I was—my actual face, my real body. I touched my cheeks, ran my fingers through my hair, patted my arms and legs, just to make sure everything was...intact.

Then, a scream—loud, uncontrollable—burst out of me. I squealed with delight, jumping up and down like a kid on a sugar high. I couldn't stop looking at myself in the mirror, grinning like an idiot. My voice—oh God, it was my voice again! I squealed louder, laughing so hard my sides hurt.

I had to check again, just to be sure. Please, please still be me. I turned back to the mirror. Yup, still the same. No weird transformations. I ran my hand through my hair—damn, it looked good. And my face—wow, my face was definitely handsome. I could barely contain myself.

Tears streamed down my face, but these weren't the sad, frustrating kind I'd known before. These were the happiest tears I'd ever cried. I was punching my pillow, pulling my hair, and laughing like a lunatic. I didn't care. I was alive. I was me.

"Yes, yes, yes—YES!" I screamed, probably loud enough to wake the entire neighbourhood.

***

Oh my God, I couldn't believe that he was truly back. I myself let out a tiny scream before I could cover my mouth. I was so so happy that Trevor was back.

Jason stirred, blinking groggily at me before rolling over and passing out again. I didn't care—I would have danced around the room if my foot wasn't still aching from the injury. The ice pack had long since melted, but nothing could dampen my mood now.

With a grin so wide it hurt, I eagerly flipped to the next page...

All of a sudden, the door swung open, and there was Mom, standing in my room with her hands on her hips. "What kind of circus is going on in here?" she scolded, her voice stern but familiar.

I looked at her—really looked at her—and for the first time in a long while, I noticed the little details I had taken for granted. The gentle lines etched around her eyes, the slight dark circles that spoke of countless nights spent working or worrying. Her face, though tired, was comforting in a way that words couldn't describe. Tears welled up in my eyes, and without thinking, I rushed toward her, wrapping my arms around her tightly.

She stiffened, clearly confused by my sudden display of affection, but I didn't care. In that moment, it hit me just how much she—and Dad—had sacrificed for me. All the late nights, the hard work, the little things they did to give me the best, while I'd been too wrapped up in my own world to notice. I buried my face into her shoulder, and for the first time, I realized just how lucky I was.

When I finally let go, she looked even more perplexed, but I was too caught up in my emotions to explain. Instead, I ran out of my room, my heart pounding with a strange mixture of joy and guilt. I found Dad sitting at the dining table, casually flipping through the newspaper. Without a word, I dashed over and hugged him from behind, my arms squeezing him tight.

He froze, clearly just as confused as Mom, and turned his head slightly, a question in his eyes. But I didn't offer any explanation. I just held him, letting my emotions wash over me. After a long moment, I let go and hurried back to my room, my head spinning with thoughts and feelings I didn't know how to process. Everything felt... new. The sun streaming through the windows seemed brighter, the world outside more alive. It was as if I was seeing it all for the first time.

And there, in his cage, was Mort. Snoring away, his little body rising and falling with each soft breath. I crouched down beside him, watching the way his round, brown-and-white cheeks puffed out as he slept. His belly expanded and contracted with each breath, his tiny paws twitching slightly. He looked so peaceful, so utterly unaware of the chaos of the world.

A wave of guilt washed over me. I remembered the day I got him—my 14th birthday. We'd gone out to that amazing Italian restaurant with my cousins, and when we got home, Mom and Dad had been grinning like they knew something I didn't. They led me into my room, and there it was—a black cage with a tiny ball of fur inside. Mort. He wasn't as chubby then, but his fur was the same perfect blend of caramel and white, his tiny ears twitching as he looked up at me with those beady black eyes.

I'd been so excited back then, rushing to name him "Mort" on the spot. I remember holding him for the first time, feeling his soft fur against my skin, staring into his curious little eyes. He had made me smile just by being there. But now, looking at him snoring away in his rusty old cage, I felt a pang of regret.

What had I done?

The cage was dirty, and I couldn't remember the last time I'd cleaned it. Maybe when it was brand new, I'd taken him out to play once or twice, but since then? I barely acknowledged him anymore. Weeks would go by without me even glancing in his direction, even though he lived right there in my room. He had become part of the background noise of my life—an afterthought.

And when I did notice him, it was often out of frustration. I used to get so annoyed with how easy his life seemed. No homework, no stress, no people making fun of him—just lounging around, eating, and sleeping. Sometimes, when I was stressed or angry, I'd take it out on him, rattling his cage or yelling at him when he made noise in the middle of the night. There were so many nights I'd just pick up his cage, put it in the hallway, and shut the door without a second thought, all because his grunting or the rattling of the cage annoyed me.

I had been a terrible owner. But now, standing there and watching him sleep so peacefully, I felt a deep sense of remorse. He deserved better than that—better than me.

Suddenly, I remembered how it felt to be stuck. How it felt to be trapped, just like I had been in that fishbowl. The helplessness, the boredom, the frustration of not being able to move or change your surroundings. And up until this moment, I had been treating Mort the same way—trapped in a tiny, dirty cage, ignored and neglected.

But it's not too late. I had another chance—to make things right, to take care of him the way he deserved. I knelt down beside the cage, whispering, "I'm sorry, buddy. I promise I'll do better."

I stared at Mort's cage, my heart sinking. There was so much dirt piled up around him, the bars rusted and stained. His fur was dusty—his once glossy, caramel-colored coat now dulled. How had I let it get this bad? Mort deserved so much better than this. I needed to fix it, clean the cage, and most of all, let him out to stretch his legs—if he could even run anymore. He looked bored, maybe even as fed up with life as I'd been.

"Hang in there, buddy. We'll get you cleaned up," I whispered, feeling guilty for neglecting him for so long.

After pulling on some fresh shorts and slipping into my flip-flops, I shouted to Mom, "I'm going for a walk!"

Her voice called back from the kitchen, "Are you okay, sweetie? Need to talk about something?"

I paused at the door, glancing back at her concerned face. "Honestly, Mom, I'm great. Couldn't be better."

She smiled, though the confusion was clear in her eyes. I waved it off, too happy to explain. For once, I wasn't weighed down by anything. I raced down the stairs, skipping the elevator entirely, the fresh morning air hitting me as soon as I stepped out into the open.

The podium area was quiet, the play area—usually full of shouting kids—stood still, bathed in the early sunlight. A few couples, just finishing their morning walks, passed by with content smiles, holding hands. I breathed in deeply, the crisp air filling my lungs. Everything seemed... brighter. More alive. The trees lining the walkway were perfectly in place, their leaves swaying gently in the breeze.

I wandered around the building, taking it all in, before stopping at the swings. Without hesitation, I hopped on and started to swing, pumping my legs back and forth, higher and higher. It felt like I was flying, weightless and free. I hadn't done this in years—how had I forgotten something so simple could be so much fun?

After ten or fifteen minutes, I reluctantly slowed down, hopping off the swing with a grin still plastered on my face. My heart wasn't full yet, though. I remembered the little ice-cream shop two blocks away, but it was probably too early for that. With a final stroll around the courtyard, I made my way back upstairs.

Mom was waiting for me at the door. Her brow furrowed slightly as she asked, "Everything alright? You're acting... different."

I grinned, shrugging lightly. "Better than ever, Mom. Just taking it all in."

Dad was getting ready to leave for work. "See you later," he said, grabbing his briefcase.

Before he could walk out, I dashed over and hugged him from behind. He froze, probably wondering what had gotten into me. I let go quickly, smiling as I waved him off. He looked back, half-confused but smiling nonetheless.

At breakfast, Mom had made my favourite—egg whites, baked beans, and toast. I sat down, giving her a grateful smile as I dug in. The first bite of crispy bacon hit my taste buds like heaven. Every bite was perfect, the baked beans pairing flawlessly with the toast. I spread the beans over the bread and took a massive bite, feeling like I was on cloud nine.

"You've really outdone yourself this morning," I said

between bites, complimenting her as I polished off my plate.

Mom watched me with a smile, clearly enjoying the sight of me devouring the food like it was the best meal I'd ever had. When I was done, she leaned in, her voice soft.

"Don't worry about that test, sweetheart. We'll figure it out. I know you worked so hard, and I'm proud of you, no matter what happens."

I looked up, meeting her warm gaze, and nodded. "Thanks, Mom."

"Dad told me about last night too," she added. "He's right. You gave it your all. Just focus on this last paper, okay? Give it your best shot."

I smiled, feeling lighter than I had in a long time. "I will, Mom. I promise."

"Oh right..." I muttered to myself, remembering last night—how I had poured my heart out to Dad, admitting everything that had been weighing on me. I nodded along, my mouth still full of food. Right, right, right—just one paper left to go. I wasn't just going to pass this test; I was going to ace it.

Determined, I stood up and mumbled, "Thanks," before heading back to my room. The calendar stared at me, three days circled in red until the final test. I glanced at the book lying on my desk, already feeling the surge of focus. I was ready—more than ready—to crush this.

After rinsing my mouth (probably should've brushed), I decided to take a hot shower. As the steam filled the bathroom, the hot water washed over me, soothing every tense muscle in my body. I let it melt away the remnants of exhaustion. Nothing beat the feeling of a fresh start—especially today.

Once dressed, I grabbed my notes and a big bottle of

water, settling down at my desk with laser focus. The hours blurred as I highlighted key terms, jotted down notes, and repeated difficult concepts to myself like I was teaching them. Time slipped away without me noticing, until Mom called me out for lunch. She poked her head into my room, smiling at the sight of papers scattered across the desk and books piled high on the bed.

"Be there in five," I replied, finishing up the chapter before closing my books.

Lunch was a brief break before I returned to my study routine. Later, when I had a little more time, I took Mort out of his cage. He had finally woken from his nap, his tiny eyes blinking slowly as I held him in the palm of my hand. His fur was rough but soft in some places, matted from neglect. I gave him a gentle scrub, carefully rubbing the dust and grease from his coat. It wasn't easy, but he looked so much better when I was done.

As I cleaned his cage, the guilt lingered—how had I ignored him for so long?

Mom had outdone herself for the next meal—pesto pasta with garlic bread. It felt like I hadn't tasted something this good in ages, and I told her as much between mouthfuls. She looked puzzled by my comment, probably because she made meals like this all the time. But today? Today it felt like a feast, and I was savoring every bite like it was the first time.

After lunch, I spent the rest of the day studying, determined to keep the momentum going. In the evening, I caught up with a couple of my friends from the building. It had been months since I'd seen most of them, and they were all a little surprised at how I was acting. I wasn't trying to make them forget anything from before—I just missed them, their company, their banter. It felt good to be around them again, and we spent an hour or so just wandering around the building, laughing and reminiscing.

When I got home, Dad had just returned from work. We had dinner together, the three of us. Dad shared some story about a last-minute save at the office, while Mom chimed in with her tales from the kitchen. I joined in, talking about the "complex problems" of my studies, and for the first time in a while, we were all laughing together at the table.

As dinner wrapped up, I suggested something we hadn't done in forever: "Can we go to the ice-cream parlor? The one we used to go to when I was a kid?"

Mom and Dad exchanged glances, surprised but excited. "Why not?" they both agreed, eager for a change of pace.

And so, after dinner, the three of us strolled down the lane to the little ice-cream shop, the evening breeze soft against our faces. Mom and Dad shared a mango cup while I indulged in my chocolate cone, savoring every lick. It had been years since we'd done something like this together, and the simple joy of it filled me with warmth.

Later that night, I stood in front of the mirror, staring at my reflection. I remembered the words I'd used to describe myself before—a sad sack of life. I couldn't believe I had ever said that. Looking at myself now, I whispered, "It's not a sad sack of life. You were the sad sack, wasting a life that's actually wonderful."

I studied my reflection—there was nothing wrong with me. Sure, I had some things to work on. But I could fix those. "We'll work on that stutter," I told myself. "We'll get into shape. A little grooming, and you'll be ready to take on the world."

I wiped away the tears that had filled my eyes, a confident smile spreading across my face. "Stop feeling sorry for yourself. Be thankful for the life you have, for the second chance you've been given. You know the value of it now. Don't even think about letting it go again. The only way forward is up."

The next two days were all about preparing for that final test. I woke up early, diving straight into my notes. I read, solved problems, and highlighted key points over and over. Barely taking breaks, I was determined to give this everything I had.

By the evening, I had covered almost everything, but there was still time left. I glanced at the PlayStation, tempted. I deserve a break, I thought, letting myself play for a little while before getting back to the books.

As I sat back down, I couldn't help but reflect on how far I'd come. From feeling like a plant trapped in a garden, to an insect barely surviving, to an animal aimlessly wandering, to a fish with nothing but time and boredom, to a mayfly with only 24 hours to live—I had been through so much. But now? Now I was back. I was human again—the most powerful, dominant creature on the planet. It was the best feeling in the world.

The sky was the limit, and I was ready to soar.

***

I quickly finished my work for the day. I spent some time cleaning Mort's cage, and it looked brand new. He seemed pretty excited to stay at the new place. I then went to sleep early. There was only one day remaining before my last paper. I prepared extremely well on the last day as well and was very confident that I would do great. Finally, it was the day of the exam. I reached the place sometime earlier. I was very relaxed and just kept on taking deep breaths.

It was time. Before I knew it, I was in the exam hall, the paper had been handed out to me and I began to write. I looked at all the questions and I let out a smile. I was really going ace this one. I was making incredible time and I was enjoying this soo much. I looked around and many of them seemed to be struggling to finish theirs. I was done with my paper almost twenty minutes before time. I let out a sigh of relief and before I knew it, the paper was out of my hands and collected by the teacher. I looked around and everyone was relieved.

Most of them were delighted and I didn't even realize it, but it was my last paper, and my exams were over. I met up with few of my friends. We made plans for lunch. I was happy. That day, I went home and told mom and dad and they too seemed very pleased. All we had to do was figure out what had to be done with the math test. The results would be given in a week. I was extremely nervous. I didn't want to fail. I mean who ever wanted to fail. I was so nervous till the day of the result. I opened up mine and to see a score of 30. I had failed the test. I couldn't believe this. Surely something had been altered. Rest of the scores were quite decent and I did extremely well in the last one.

Surprisingly, Dad walked into the room, a smile playing on his lips. He had that look—the one that told me something unexpected was coming. He paused at the door, arms crossed, and gave me a smirk.

"Guess what?" he began, letting the words hang in the air for a moment. "You got one more chance for that test of yours."

I shot up from my seat, eyes wide in disbelief. "Wait, the math one?" I asked, my voice a mix of shock and excitement.

Dad nodded, still smiling. "Yes, the math one. The coordinator noticed the improvement in your other scores, and apparently, a few other students had the same issue with the difficulty level of the last paper. So, they're giving you another shot."

I couldn't believe it. Relief flooded over me. "Are you serious?" I asked, trying to contain the surge of hope rising in my chest.

"Dead serious," he replied, still smirking. "Two weeks from now. You've got time to prepare and ace it this time."

A wave of determination hit me. I smiled back at him, feeling a renewed sense of purpose. "I won't let you down, Dad," I promised.

"That's my boy," he said, ruffling my hair before leaving the room.

Well, what can I say next, I studied so hard for this test, like the previous one felt like nothing. The amount of effort, this wasn't just to ace the test, this was to prove myself and I can accomplish whatever I set my mind to. I just kept on studying hard for the next two weeks, just loads and loads of solving and practice and revision. And what can I say, I aced it.

Mom and dad were so happy with what they were seeing. They were genuinely surprised as to what had caused this change. Like it was a complete 360 degree to what they had witnessed and seen. I couldn't explain what I had witnessed in the last days. I myself couldn't believe what was going on. It slowly started clicking, one by one, just understanding the various importance in each case. Well, I was just happy that I was being the best version of me.

I would just wake up in the morning and just thank God for the place that I was put in, thank God for my life, thank God for my food, my shelter, my clothing and after practicing gratitude, I would just be in a splendid mood. All these tensions, negativity was just a blip in this beautiful canvass of life.

The next part of it is so great. It seemed like a fairytale but all it really was, was a mixture of hard work, gratitude, patience, love and confidence. I could write a completely new book on the next stages of my life but it seems like a beautiful ending to this roller coaster of a journey and so I feel even a couple of pages would do the trick.

I spent the next year and a half of my high school just simply trying to become the best version of myself. I worked on my stutter. I would book regular appointments with my speech therapist, and she would come over to my place about twice a week. One-hour sessions each and about a couple of months, I was almost perfect. Not only did my stutter almost went away, but I was also feeling so much more confident than before. I even lost a lot of weight. I lost like 30 pounds in about 3 months. And I got really into fitness.

I joined a gym which was like ten minutes walking from my place. The atmosphere was electric over there. There were people of all kinds. Some looked like chiseled wax statues, some in a worse shape than me, some elderly people as well. It was simply amazing. I really loved going to the gym. My entire lifestyle had drastically changed, a complete 180 to be honest. I was eating right, sleeping right, I met a lot of new people, they inspired me so much.

Everyone had their own stories to tell. Especially these two guys named Hank and Simon. They really helped me a lot in pushing myself to the limit. They treated me like I was one of them. Both of them had been working out for a couple of years. They gave me a lot of tips on my diet, my workout routines and helped me a lot in correcting posture. I was able to grow very quickly in terms of strength. I went to the gym for about three times a week. I only ate home food which was absolutely yummy.

I worked hard every single day, be it the schoolwork, or on my personal self. We even decided to shift from the place we were staying. The work at the new place was actually going on for a while now. But it was about 45 minutes from this place.

It was an up-and-coming neighbourhood, and we would be living in a proper house, with a front porch and a backyard and all that stuff. It was going to be great; it was going to be different. I was looking forward to it. I mean this place was alright, but I think with all of this I was ready to move to a new chapter. After a couple of months, beginning of the new academic year, we finally shifted out from that old place. The hall was painted with a mix of pastel shades of purple, blue and white. The interiors were done up so well. The couch looked lovely. It was simply stunning. The entire hall was very spacious.

I loved the new house. It was simply stunning. The neighborhood had this lively, welcoming vibe. A lot of new families had just moved in, and there was a small fair happening right outside. I found myself stepping out more often, enjoying the fresh air, and even made a couple of friends from the area. We'd hang out in our free time, just exploring the place.

At school, people started noticing my change too. It was funny to watch the reaction from those who never gave me a second glance before. Of course, there were still a few spoiled brats who were too proud to talk to me. Fine by me, I thought. If they wanted to, they would. And anyway, next year, the batches would change, and with any luck, I wouldn't have to see their smug faces again.

Our school was massive—ten divisions for each grade. So, every year, you'd only see a couple of familiar faces. Honestly, I didn't care anymore. Life had a way of sifting out the people that mattered. Speaking of which, I still had a crush on Rose. We spoke more frequently now—sometimes texting, sometimes calling. It felt... good.

Before I knew it, the end-of-semester exams rolled around. I was confident, prepared, and it paid off. I scored an overall A grade, and with a three-month break ahead, I was determined to make the most of it.

Over the break, I threw myself into self-improvement. My final session with my speech therapist was a triumph. I spoke so fluently, articulating every word with precision. It was hard to believe that I'd ever had a stutter in the first place. My therapist and I were both ecstatic. I was so grateful to her, and more than that, I was proud of myself. I didn't hesitate in conversations anymore. I didn't shy away from speaking. People seemed more approachable, and I didn't take crap from anyone. I could fire back with ease and stand my ground.

Physically, I was transforming too. Six months of eating clean and going to the gym had paid off—I'd lost fifty pounds. My body had changed completely. I was taller, leaner, and my overall physique was night and day from what it used to be. It was like my life had fallen into place just by taking that first step of dedication. I even installed a basketball hoop in the backyard and spent hours shooting hoops. Sometimes, friends would join in, and before we knew it, the day had slipped away.

I also took time to explore what I really wanted to do. Science wasn't my thing—I knew that much. But architecture? Now that was something that intrigued me. I'd always been good at drawing and design. It felt like my jam. Music, too, had a special place in my heart. I'd learned to play the guitar and sing, but I wasn't entirely sure about pursuing it professionally. Summer was about figuring that out.

In between, we went on a family trip. It was amazing—kayaking, snorkeling, trekking. The food was incredible, probably some of the best meals I'd ever had. The trek was about two hours, and it was more fun than I had expected. I even picked up a few new hobbies. All in all, the trip was a great success.

But not everything was sunshine. The sad part was, Mort passed away. He had been with me for three and a half years—longer than most of his kind live. He got sick, and the next day, he wasn't moving. I felt a surge of guilt for neglecting him for nearly two years. But I took some solace in knowing that I did my best to make his last days more comfortable. Still, I cried. It hit harder than I thought it would.

During that time, Rose and I became close friends. We

stayed in touch, and we even decided to volunteer at a nearby soup kitchen. It felt good to do something meaningful together, and, honestly, it didn't hurt that it would look good on college applications too. I'll never forget the first time she saw me post-transformation.

"Woah... I mean, you look completely different. New haircut?" she asked, her eyes wide in surprise.

"A new everything," I replied with a smile.

We spent two hours daily at the soup kitchen, from 5 to 7 in the evening. It was rewarding work. There's something about handing over a warm meal to someone who truly needs it. I knew the value of food, probably more than most. Seeing the gratitude in their eyes made all the hard work worth it.

There was always something to do—cleaning, fetching vegetables, cooking, washing dishes. Sometimes we'd just be cleaning up long after everyone had left. But it felt right, like we were making a difference. It wasn't just about the soup; it was about giving people hope, even if it was just for a moment.

Through all this, I couldn't help but reflect on my journey. The kid I used to be? He seemed like a distant memory. This wasn't just a change in appearance or attitude; it was a change in heart. And for the first time in a long time, I was truly proud of the person I was becoming.

CHAPTER 14

UNSTOPPABLE

A month flew by in a blur, and before I realized it, school was set to start in just a week. Looking back on the vacation, it was easily one of the best I'd had in years. The freedom, the self-discovery—it all left me feeling energized. Then, almost in the blink of an eye, it was the first day of 12th grade.

By the time I walked into school, I was in the best shape of my life—stronger, more muscular, and confident in ways I hadn't been before. It felt like I had been reborn, yet the place was still familiar, though strangely different. I couldn't recall many good memories of my time here, but I was damn sure that was about to change.

Walking into the new classroom, I scanned the faces—most of them were new. Not many of my 11th-grade classmates had ended up here, but that was fine by me. I spotted an empty seat in the middle row, next to a blonde-haired guy.

"Hey, mind if I sit here?" I asked, my voice casual.

"Sure," he replied, not looking up from his notebook.

Well, that wasn't hard, I thought to myself as I slid into the seat. Still, I couldn't help but feel a twinge of disappointment that Rose and I weren't in the same class. It meant we wouldn't see each other as much, and with new classes, new teachers, and new friends, I knew it would be tough to stay close. Our school was massive—it could be weeks before we even bumped into each other.

Despite that, I quickly fell into a groove. Before long, I'd made a tight group of friends, and by the end of the first semester, there were eight of us who stuck together. I stayed focused in lectures, finished my assignments on time, and even my teachers seemed shocked by the new version of me. Some of them had known me in 11th grade, and the look on their faces said it all—they couldn't believe the transformation.

And speaking of transformations, I was in the sweet spot of my gym routine. After six months of consistent workouts, I was in great shape—no more weight to lose, just intense training and lifting. Each gym session left me exhausted, but it was the kind of exhaustion that came with satisfaction. Every Saturday night, my group of friends and I would play basketball on the court—us versus the guys from the opposite block. It was a blast, and I always looked forward to it.

Those six months flew by so fast, but I enjoyed every moment. And even more than that, I started to realize how much I loved architecture. I'd always had a knack for drawing, and math had quickly become my strong suit. I was thinking seriously about becoming an architect. Sometimes my friends would get bored because I'd go on and on about building layouts or designs whenever we were out. Whether we were eating at a restaurant or riding the metro, I'd catch myself analyzing the structures, and they'd just laugh or roll their eyes.

One night, I remember we were at this Italian restaurant,

and I was stuffed after my second serving of chicken noodles. It was around 7 PM, and the sky was breathtaking—swirls of orange, red, and purple that looked like they belonged in a painting. After we paid the bill, we stepped outside and took a stroll down the sidewalk. The wind was gentle, brushing past us as we walked under the vibrant evening sky.

As we passed by a glass building, I froze in my tracks. The design, the sleekness of it, stirred something in me—a memory. I was about six years old, perched on my dad's shoulders as we left the cinema. We had taken a walk afterward, and I remember staring up at a spiralling tower, its shiny mirrors catching the last rays of sunlight, its sharp edges standing out against the sky. I was mesmerized then, just as I was now.

It was the same building, standing in the same spot after all these years. That memory hit me like a freight train—this was the first time I'd ever thought about creating something of my own. I didn't even know the word "architect" back then, but I knew I wanted to build something like that tower. And now, years later, that memory had come flooding back.

I stood there, lost in thought, the childhood version of myself resurfacing—wide-eyed, full of curiosity and awe. It was a feeling I hadn't experienced in years. After all the self-doubt, the pity, the constant beating down of my own mind, this memory was like a breath of fresh air. A tear welled up in my eye, but it wasn't sadness—it was relief. It was a moment of clarity I hadn't expected.

I must've been standing there for a while because suddenly I heard my name being called. My friends had walked ahead, and someone had finally noticed I was missing. I looked back at the building one last time and whispered, "Thank you."

I wasn't sure why I felt compelled to say it, but I knew this was a moment I'd carry with me for the rest of my life.

"Welcome back," I whispered to myself, grinning as I caught up with my friends. They were probably wondering what had gotten into me, but I didn't care. Moments like this, the ones that touch you in an unexpected way, they're the ones you never forget.

After about an hour of wandering around, we all split up and headed home. As soon as I walked through the door, I told my parents about the building, the memory of that day, and how everything just felt right. I had finally found something I was passionate about—architecture. Their faces lit up with proud smiles. It felt good, knowing that I had their support. Within weeks, I started working on my applications, and in two months, everything was done.

But just as I had predicted, Rose and I lost touch. At first, we texted or called every few days, then it became weeks, and now… it had been almost a month. Life pulled us into different worlds. That's just how it was, I suppose.

The rest of the days passed in a blur of gym sessions and classes, and I grew physically stronger each month. Schoolwork was right on track, too. But there's one moment I know I'll never forget. It was December—my birthday, to be exact.

I usually took the day off on my birthday, just because I liked having it to myself. But this time, I had to go in for an English quiz. I figured I'd sit through it and then leave early. The plan was simple: sneak out after the quiz and enjoy the rest of the day.

A few of us decided to cut class after the second lecture. We had to be careful—teachers patrolled the corridors like hawks.

As the bell rang, we slipped out of the classroom and darted down the hallway, hearts pounding with the thrill of getting away with it.

Just as I turned the corner, I slammed into someone. Hard.

"Watch it!" I blurted out, only to realize who I'd run into. Not Rose, not a teacher—worse. It was Christian, my childhood bully. His sneer hit me before his words did.

"Well, well, look who it is," he drawled, eyeing me up and down. "Think you're some kind of tough guy now?"

"Sorry, man, I didn't see you—" I started, but he cut me off, stepping closer.

"I didn't see you... I didn't see you..." he mimicked, pushing me hard in the chest. I stumbled back.

My friends froze, unsure of what to do, but I wasn't scared. Not anymore.

"Look, I said I'm sorry. Just let it go," I warned him, my voice calm but firm.

"Or what?" Christian's smirk widened. "You think you're something now? Just 'cause you lost a few pounds, you think you're tough?"

He shoved me again—this time with both hands—and I nearly lost my balance. That was it. I saw red. Without thinking, I charged at him, throwing my full weight into a shove that sent him sprawling to the floor.

The hallway erupted with chants of "Fight! Fight! Fight!"

I stood over him, fists clenched, breathing hard. "Stay away from me," I growled.

For a second, I thought that was it—that I'd scared him enough. But he scrambled to his feet, fury in his eyes, and took a swing at me, landing a punch square on my jaw. Pain shot through my face, but I didn't back down. My friends surged forward, but I raised my hand, stopping them.

This was between me and Christian.

He came at me again, another wild punch, but this time I ducked. The crowd gasped, a chorus of "Oooohs" echoing through the hallway. Without hesitating, I drove my knee into his stomach, hard. He doubled over, clutching his ribs.

Years of anger, humiliation, and frustration boiled over. I made a fist, as tight as I could, and threw a right hook straight into his cheek. Christian dropped like a sack of potatoes, hitting the ground with a sickening thud. My knuckles throbbed, but I didn't care.

I wasn't done yet.

I straddled him, pinning his arms beneath my knees. His face, once smug and arrogant, was now twisted in fear. This was for all the years of torment—for every time he humiliated me, embarrassed me, made me feel worthless.

Just as I raised my fist to land another blow, Christian's voice broke through the chants.

"HELP!" he screamed, tears streaming down his face. He was sobbing, begging for mercy.

I hesitated, looking down at him—a cowardly, crying mess. A part of me wanted to laugh at how pathetic he looked, but I just shook my head. I didn't feel any pity for him. Not yet. I punched him one last time, landing a solid hit to his nose, which started bleeding.

That's when the teachers arrived. My friends dragged me off Christian, who lay there whimpering in a pool of his own blood. I couldn't help it—I laughed. A full, chest-shaking laugh. It was my first fight, and it felt damn good to finally stand up to that jerk.

I was still laughing when they hauled us both to the principal's office. Christian was taken to the nurse, and I was given a lengthy lecture. Detention for me. But honestly? It was worth it. All we talked about afterward was the fight. My mind kept replaying the scene over and over. Yeah, it was a hell of a birthday.

When I got home and told my parents what had happened, they were furious. Even though it was my birthday, I was sent straight to my room. I sulked, thinking they'd understand, but nope.

Later, as I sat playing PlayStation, my dad knocked and walked in.

"Come on," he said, his tone soft. "Let's go out for dinner. That Italian place you like... it's still your birthday, after all. Get dressed, we'll leave in fifteen."

Before he shut the door, he poked his head back in, a grin on his face. "Did you win?"

I smirked back. "Of course."

Turns out, the school had called my parents earlier, and they were required to meet with the principal the next day. But that was a problem for future me. For now, I had won, and that was enough.

The next day at school, Mom came with me to talk to the vice principal. I was on the verge of suspension, and I knew that my turnaround in grades and the rapport I had built with my teachers probably saved me from the worst outcome. In the end, I was let off with two days of detention.

But honestly? It was worth it. I would do it all over again. That turned out to be the only fight during my last year at that school. Sure, I'd gotten into a scuffle during my third year of college, but it was nothing compared to this. Beating my childhood bully a year after finally standing up to him? Nothing could beat that.

The rest of twelfth grade flew by, and soon we were just months away from finals. Everything went smoothly, and I managed to balance my workload with gym time, family, and friends, though it got hectic, leaving me exhausted most days. Despite that, I still did well.

To top it all off, I received conditional offers from three of the five colleges I had applied to. My parents were thrilled, and before I knew it, it was time for our farewell. I really enjoyed the event, and the afterparty was a blast. It took place at a friend's house, and the entire day was superb. Exams were just around the corner, but we all agreed to hang out until they were over. Those days flew by, and they were some of the most amazing times of my life. I still couldn't believe it all happened just a year ago; no one could have imagined this change.

The next three weeks were a blur of study sessions. I buried myself in my books, but when the exams were over, it was finally vacation time. I received a text from Rose that I hadn't properly responded to, and we decided to meet up.

I bumped into her outside the exam hall for our design paper, and it felt strange to see her there after all this time. I'd been wanting to tell her how I felt since we first met, but the fear of rejection had always held me back. After the exam, I finally mustered the courage to ask her to talk privately. We chatted about the paper, then I took a deep breath.

"Rose, I need to tell you something. I've had feelings for

you for a while now. You've always been so kind, and... would you like to go out for dinner after exams?"

There was a pause, her eyes wide with surprise. "Yes," she whispered softly. I felt my heart leap with joy as I replied, "Can't wait," before we parted ways.

Our dinner was wonderful, just a couple of blocks from school. We talked about everything under the sun, and the atmosphere was beautiful. I had never imagined that this day would turn out like this. She shared her ambitions of pursuing a career in product design, and I revealed my plans for architecture. We spoke about college applications, memories from school, and how different things used to be.

"Can you believe we're actually graduating?" I asked, smiling.

"I know, right? It feels surreal," she replied, her eyes sparkling.

As the evening wore on, we learned that this was our last chance to connect before the world pulled us in different directions. She'd be visiting her grandparents in Canada, while I'd head to Texas to see my cousins.

The night ended too soon, and I found myself standing outside her place. "Thanks for today," she said softly, her eyes shining. Then, she leaned in and gave me a gentle peck on the cheek, turning away with a charming smile as she walked toward the door. I stood there, grinning like an idiot, savoring the moment. This was one I'd always cherish.

Well, I was lucky to say I had even greater things ahead. I met the love of my life, the woman who would become my wife, I got accepted into NYU, and the packing began.

Everything was confirmed, and I would be leaving home

within a month. I spent quality time with my parents, who spoiled me a bit. We ate at every place I wanted, enjoying the tastiest food. My friends also received acceptances to great colleges, and just like that, the farewell party for our batch was a fantastic reunion.

We all cherished this time together before life took us on different paths. I was genuinely going to miss this place, despite moving to a new neighborhood. The upcoming area was beautiful—a proper house with a front porch and a backyard.

We shifted to the new house, and let me tell you, I loved it. It was stunning. The neighborhood was vibrant, filled with new families, and there was a small fair outside. I started getting out more often, making friends from the neighborhood and hanging out with them.

But there were still a few spoiled brats who thought they were too good to talk to me. Fine by me. They would learn soon enough. Anyway, next year, the batches would change. I wouldn't have to see their smug faces again, hopefully.

As for Rose, she was still on my mind. We'd shared a connection, and I hoped to rekindle that.

The rest of the year rushed by, and before I knew it, it was almost time for our exams. I had been focused, balancing my studies and my social life, and it all seemed to pay off.

In the first semester, I had managed to keep my grades up while enjoying life. There were ups and downs, but every moment felt like a victory.

Fast forward to December, and I had received three offers from the colleges I applied to. Everything felt like a whirlwind, but I was grateful for the journey I had taken to get here.

As the year wrapped up, I felt hopeful for what lay ahead.

The past year, with all its challenges and uncertainties, had finally come to an end. Looking forward, I saw a future free from fear, a world brimming with endless possibilities. I knew I had to strive to become the best version of myself, keep my mind and body fit, pursue my passion with all my might, and, above all, enjoy the entire process.

Before I knew it, the day of leaving had finally arrived. I was ready to go, and I was ready for whatever was in store for me. After all the bags were loaded, my parents gave me a tight hug. "Take care son," replied my dad. My mom was almost in tears. I hugged them and I was going to miss them a lot. I could see their last goodbyes, as I proceeded to enter the airport. I was ready for everything. I looked down at the tiny buildings as the plane took off; the boarding pass in my coat pocket, a bag of Doritos in my hand, headphones on and I was ready to take on this college by storm…

CHAPTER 15

EXPERIENCES

The first day at college was something altogether different. It was a humongous place with thousands of students swarming all over. I thought my school was big, this was at a whole new level. There was chaos all over. People were chattering nearby, folders were flying around, registration lines were growing long, and people were cramming inside.

After finishing all the formalities, I finally got the key to my dorm. I grabbed my suitcase and reached the place. I looked around and it seemed alright, I guess. There were two small cupboards, two beds a few feet away from each other. We even had a washroom to ourselves as well, which was great. Overall, I was getting a positive vibe from the place, which was good, considering I had to spend the next four years of my life over here.

The other bed was still empty, so I guess my roommate hadn't still come yet. I just kept all my stuff down and unpacked my bag on the nearest of the two beds. I sat down; relaxed for a bit and then went to the nearby washroom. I was living in a contrast of emotions. On the one hand, I had my expectations quite high from college and I wanted to have a complete blast and felt so good being on my own and on the other hand, I was missing the life that I had lived till exactly a few hours earlier.

I unpacked some of my stuff and went down to grab some food. It was almost dinner time. Orientation week would be beginning from tomorrow and regular lectures would start in a week's time. The entire place looked very beautiful but for some reason everyone already had their little groups and I found it a bit difficult to fit in. I didn't think too much of it. The next couple of days I did manage to make a couple of friends and before I knew it, I was at my first college party.

It was the same weekend and there were like around thirty people in the common room and the dorm area. The music was going on at full blast. There was a curfew, and everyone had to be back in their dorm latest by 11. It was already around two in the night. There was need for some more drinks and people were too chickened out to do it, so a guy named Philip and I set out for to get it at the nearest store which was a couple of blocks away from college.

It was pitch dark outside and somehow, we managed to reach the store and brought back some of the drinks in a white cloth bag. We were just a few feet away from the campus main door when some guard shouted "HEY! WHAT ARE YOU GUYS DOING OUT HERE!!" and that sudden voice startled both of us. We got so panicked we didn't' know what to do. The other dude just sprinted within seconds leaving me with the bag. It took me a few seconds to understand what to do. I was completely confused. Within the next few seconds, even I took a run from it—I had to carry the bag. If the security guard found it, there would be a huge investigation and things would get way worse. For now, I had to just escape him.

I entered the main lobby; I began to climb the staircase and I could feel him right at my tiptoes. I entered the second floor and was trying to find another way to get out from here, but I reached a dead end. I was just a couple of feet away from my room, but I could not find my keys. Like an idiot, I left my keys at the dorm room where the party was going on. I could hear his loud footsteps approaching. I was trying to figure out a way of exiting the place when all of a sudden, I felt a door open next to me and felt a strong tug and I was pushed into the room – my own room!

There was a tall guy standing in front of me, thick black and piercing blue eyes. He had a hint of a moustache and a light stubble. He just looked at me, and just signaled me to stay where I was. He was still in his outside clothes, dark blue jeans and a t-shirt, jacket, and everything, a brown-coloured handbag still on his shoulder. He went outside slowly in a calm and relaxed manner. A few seconds later, I heard another pair of footsteps and realized the guard was standing outside too.

A bunch of words were exchanged, and I was patiently listening as the two of them were talking in a quiet, composed tone. I remained frozen at the spot; I could hear my own heartbeat. I was still in a state of fear and was so worried that he was going to forcibly come inside if he wasn't convinced. I looked around and yes, it was my own room, the same dorm that I lived in. I could see all my clothes scattered on the back and my laptop on the desk. My Michael Jordan poster lay firmly stuck onto the sidewall. I then saw a bunch of suitcases lying on the other side of the bed.

I could hear one pair of footsteps retreating, then silence. The door creaked open, and it was the same guy from earlier. "Don't worry, he's gone. And he won't be coming back," he said, offering a reassuring smile.

"Name's Benjamin. I actually just got here a little while ago. I'm new to this place and enrolled in the Computer Science program."

I exhaled, finally feeling the tension leave my body. "Well, I'm Trevor. Believe it or not, I'm your roommate. I'm in the architecture course, and all this stuff"—I gestured to the clothes scattered around the room—"it's mine. Thought for a second you weren't going to show up." I shook his hand firmly. "Hey, thanks for the save. I owe you big time."

"No problem," he replied, smirking. "Just show me around campus, and we'll call it even."

"Done," I said with a grin.

Little did I know then, standing there in our cramped dorm room, that Benjamin, with his strange animal-skin boots and laid-back attitude, would someday be the best man at my wedding and the godfather to my children. That was how I met one of my closest friends—someone who'd be by my side through it all. We ended up spending the rest of that night talking, getting to know each other, and before long, we were roommates and friends for life.

***

My college experience was nothing short of a blast. I made lifelong friends, had a fantastic group of people around me, and loved every minute of my architecture course. Each day was a new adventure—challenging, fun, and exciting.

One of my proudest moments came at the end of my second year. I was on the college basketball team, which was one of the top teams in the entire tri-state area. We dominated in most competitions, consistently proving ourselves as the team to beat.

Though we narrowly missed out on a few trophies, our reputation was solid. Several players had gone professional after their college days, and two even played at the national level last year.

I never had aspirations to go pro, but basketball was my passion. Competing in these tournaments was exhilarating. However, the pinnacle of college basketball was the I-League, a six-month-long tournament featuring more than 50 colleges. It was the most coveted title, one we had missed twice, always losing to our arch-rivals, Columbia University.

This year, we had something to prove. We breezed through to the semi-finals, thrashing our opponents 85-68. The semis, though, were a nail-biter. We trailed Fordham by 8 points heading into the 4th quarter. Just when things looked bleak, our point guard pulled off two back-to-back threes, followed by a brilliant steal that led to an easy lay-up. We managed to edge out a victory by 1 point, narrowly avoiding overtime.

The finals were set, and our nemesis, Columbia, stood in our way once again. Game day arrived, and we were a mix of excitement and nerves. The entire college turned out to support us—the stands were packed not just with students but also professors, alumni, and even the Dean himself. The atmosphere was electric.

We started strong. Our shots were falling, and everything was going according to plan. But Columbia wasn't backing down; they capitalized on every opportunity they got. The game swung back and forth, both teams fighting tooth and nail. Tensions ran high.

Then, disaster struck. Paxton, one of our key players, was driving to the baseline for a layup when Columbia's bulky center slammed into him mid-air. Paxton crashed to the floor with a sprained ankle and a bruised arm. The entire arena fell silent.

Our momentum wavered. Paxton was a critical player for us, and his injury threw off our rhythm. But we couldn't afford to lose focus now—not with everything on the line. We rallied together, determined to finish what we started.

The moment Paxton went down, chaos erupted on the court. We all rushed to his side, but the floor was soon flooded with players, coaches, and staff. Tensions were high, and it felt like any second, fists might fly. I was ready to defend my teammate, but before things got out of hand, we were pulled apart by the staff. After a few heated exchanges, the refs finally calmed things down. The best they could do was give Columbia's center a technical foul, though it didn't feel like justice considering Paxton was limping with a messed-up arm and ankle.

Paxton, determined, hobbled to the baseline to take his free throws. The pain was visible on his face, and he missed both shots. Immediately, he was subbed out. His absence hit us hard, and we let a few crucial plays slip, costing us valuable points. By the end of the third quarter, we were trailing by six, and the game felt like it was slipping away.

We regrouped during a timeout. Our coach knew we had to change the tempo if we had any hope of turning things around. He pushed me and our point guard forward, instructing us to apply full pressure on their guards and disrupt their flow. Behind us, the defence formed a tight triangle, determined not to let anyone past. The strategy paid off. We managed two steals in quick succession, and I converted both into points, drawing a foul on one play. Suddenly, we were just one point behind.

As the final minute ticked down, the tension in the arena was palpable. The crowd was on its feet, the noise deafening. Then, Columbia hit a clutch three-pointer, putting us four points behind with just 45 seconds left. Instead of panicking, we slowed the game down, carefully picking our moment. A quick slip by their defense gave us an easy layup. Now, we were only two points behind.

"Defence! defence! defence!" the crowd chanted, urging us on. Columbia was rattled. Our power forward intercepted a pass, diving for the ball and securing possession. I jumped into the air, pumping my fists. The coach called another timeout. Ten seconds left. Two points down. Our ball.

We huddled up, going over the final play. The atmosphere was electric, everyone on edge. The game resumed, and the clock started ticking. Our shooting guard received the inbound pass, immediately swarmed by defenders. He couldn't get a clean shot and fumbled the ball. It bounced into my hands, with only four seconds left. Without thinking, I spun to the right, two defenders charging at me. With barely any time to set, I took a fading three-pointer.

The buzzer sounded as the ball was still in the air. We

all hit the floor hard, tangled in bodies. Then I heard it—the sweetest sound a basketball player could hear. Swoosh! The ball sailed cleanly through the net.

The arena exploded in cheers. The noise was overwhelming as my teammates rushed me, lifting me into the air. We had won by one point. On the buzzer. It was surreal. Hugs, pats on the back, cheers—it all felt like a dream. We had done it. We had brought the I-League trophy home, avenging the last two years of losses to Columbia.

That memory is etched in my mind, one of those rare moments you replay again and again, always with a smile. Moments like those stand the test of time.

***

That summer of my third year, I got my first taste of professional life. It was a dream internship at Walthouse Design, a renowned architectural firm. The project I worked on was monumental—the redevelopment of the New York Public Library. Anyone familiar with the city knows the importance of that building, both in its architecture and its cultural significance.

I was beyond excited to be a part of something so massive, even though my position was temporary. The team welcomed me like one of their own, and I quickly found my footing. The boss and my supervisor were incredibly kind, always open to my ideas, even though I was just an intern. I poured everything into my work, contributing wherever I could. They noticed my creativity and praised my contributions, which only fueled my passion.

Each morning, I woke up excited to go to work. The office environment was dynamic, and time flew by. Before I knew it, two months had passed, and my internship came to an end. It was my first experience in a professional setting, and contrary to the horror stories you often hear, it was a blast. It confirmed what I had always known—this was the career I was meant for.

Those two months shaped my future in ways I couldn't have imagined, and the lessons I learned went beyond architecture. It was about teamwork, dedication, and realizing that when you love what you do, work never really feels like work.

***

College life and Internship was definitely a rollercoaster, with its share of highs and lows. I had a lot of fun—studying, making friends, attending parties, and getting involved in all sorts of activities. But no matter how great it was, I couldn't help but miss home. It took me a while to fully adjust to the college lifestyle. The food at the cafeteria was decent, but it lacked that special touch. There's something about home-cooked meals, the warmth in every bite, that you just can't replicate. Nothing ever quite measured up to that.

Being away from family was tough, though. I only got to visit home twice a year, and although living on my own had its perks, the solitude was always there. I had to do everything myself—laundry, grocery shopping, cooking when I wanted something other than cafeteria food. There was no one to whip up a snack when I was hungry or make my favorite comfort dish when I was feeling down.

It was a learning curve, though, and college taught me more than just what was in the textbooks. I picked up life skills I never thought I'd need. Before college, I hadn't so much as boiled water, but by the end of my first year, I could cook a decent meal. They weren't gourmet dishes by any stretch, but they were good enough to keep me going. And when I got sick, I learned to look after myself—there was no one to bring me soup or fuss over me like Mom would.

The hardest part, though, was dealing with setbacks on my own. If I scored low on a project or didn't do as well as I hoped in an exam, there was no one to lift me up. I had to dig deep, motivate myself, and keep pushing forward. But that's what college does to you—it shapes you, makes you stronger, more resilient. It teaches you how to stand on your own two feet, how to cope when things don't go your way.

Looking back, it was this phase that made me tough. It wasn't just about academics or making friends; it was about growing into a more capable, independent person. And that's an essential part of everyone's life—the part where you stop relying on others and start building yourself up, brick by brick.

CHAPTER 16

LOVE

Without even realizing it, the years of college flew by, and suddenly I found myself with only six months left when I spotted her—the prettiest girl waiting in line at the canteen. She had the most mesmerizing hazel brown eyes that sparkled in the light, perfectly complementing her hair color. Dressed in a bottle green sweatshirt, black cargo pants, and matching shoes, her style mirrored mine, which caught me off guard.

Immediately, I was taken aback. I had never seen her before until now. She carried a tiny backpack, and in her hands were a couple of large, rolled-up charts—no way, she had to be an architecture student! She was sitting alone, and after she had settled at one of the nearby tables, I mustered up the courage to walk over and introduce myself.

"Hey, I'm Trevor," I said, flashing my most charming smile.

"Hi, I'm Lily," she replied, her smile brightening up the room. "I'm from New York."

As we talked, I learned that she was a third-year student—just one year below me—and shared my dream of becoming a renowned architect right here in New York. I watched her animatedly talk about her passion and her journey, and I found myself completely captivated. It felt as though we had known each other for years, not just moments.

Before I knew it, an hour had passed, and I realized I was late for class. But I didn't want to leave without getting her number. "Can I have your number? I'd love to hang out again."

"Sure!" she replied, and I smiled as I saved her number in my phone. "It was great meeting you."

"Likewise, Lily. See you soon!"

Awww, this was so cute. I always wanted to know how my parents met; I made a mental note to ask them later.

As I headed to class, I couldn't shake the warm feeling in my chest. "Well, that was something. I haven't felt this way in a long, long time," I thought, smiling to myself. Over the next few weeks, we hung out when we could, getting to know each other better. I adored her personality; she was genuine, funny, and passionate about her work, but we were both so busy with assignments and classes.

After completing one of my major projects, I decided to ask her out for dinner. When she said "yes," I was ecstatic. We had a fantastic time at the restaurant, discovering a shared love for food. It turned out she was an even bigger foodie than I was, and like me, she loved trying new dishes.

We made it a point to meet every few days, often keeping it simple. Usually, it was grabbing something quick at the canteen or heading to a nearby ice cream shop for our favorite treats. She was a big fan of vanilla, while I stuck to my all-time favorite—chocolate.

But as the semester progressed, it was time to get serious.

With only a couple of months left and recruitment for companies beginning, we had a lot on our plates. One of the highlights of my college experience was securing the job I had always wanted at Walthouse Design—the very firm that inspired me to pursue architecture.

Yes! I was over the moon! I had aimed for four to five different firms, but my heart was set on Walthouse. After successfully clearing the aptitude test for three of them, I received offers from two companies.

When the news came through, my heart raced. "This is it, my first real job at one of the best firms in the world!" I shouted in excitement, unable to contain my joy.

"Wow, Trevor! That's amazing!" Lily exclaimed when I shared the news with her later. The glow in her eyes made my heart soar.

As graduation approached, I knew this was just the beginning of a thrilling chapter in my life, and I was grateful to have someone like Lily by my side as I embarked on this journey.

I was over the moon. Celebrating with all my friends, most of whom had also landed good jobs, was the perfect way to kick off this new chapter. As soon as I got the news, I called my parents, and they were thrilled. We went out that weekend and partied like there was no tomorrow, enjoying every bit of it.

The next day, I met Lily to share the news. She was so excited for me, and her bone-crushing hug made it all the more special. Everything felt like it was falling into place. All that was left was to ace these final exams, and my college days would officially be over. Lily and I went out a few more times, and before we knew it, we were actually dating—although we hadn't officially said the words yet. It was just happening, and it felt perfect.

Benjamin and I made plans to rent an apartment together near campus since he had also landed a job in New York. We already knew each other well, and living together seemed like an easy choice.

Before I knew it, exams were done. I felt a sense of relief but also a bit of sadness because, with that, my time at college had come to an end. The graduation party was beautiful and emotional. I'll never forget the speeches—everyone was crying, including me. It was a bittersweet moment, realizing we were all moving on to different stages of our lives.

Lily and I met up after everything had settled. Most of our friends were either moving away or continuing to live in the city. The day before I moved out of the dorms, Lily and I had a long talk. We decided to continue dating since I'd be living close by, and what we had was too good to let go. Moving into the new apartment with Benjamin was hectic, but once everything was in place, we were both excited to start this new chapter.

After settling in, I flew back home for some quality time with my parents before my job started. It felt great to be back, and we spent those few days reconnecting. I encouraged them to visit me in New York once I had settled into the job, promising to take them out when they did.

Returning to New York for my first day of work was surreal. Many of my colleagues remembered me from my internship, and it felt like a warm welcome back. However, the work life was intense. Days turned into weeks, and before I knew it, months had passed. I was completely immersed in my job, barely having time for anything else.

Eventually, I told my parents about Lily. I made it clear that while we were both happy, we were prioritizing our careers for the time being and weren't sure what the future held. Lily and I were doing well, but the demands of our jobs were starting to take a toll. Then one day, out of the blue, she showed up at my building with some amazing news—she had landed a job at Alanya Firms, another top architecture company in New York. We were both ecstatic! The firm was about 45 minutes away, which meant we were still close enough to see each other frequently.

A few months after she started working, we found her a place not too far from my apartment. Despite the craziness of our schedules, things were going great. And as fate would have it, Lily turned out to be the one. After two or three more years of dating, we decided to get married.

I'll never forget the night I proposed. It was a freezing winter evening, and we had just finished a lovely meal at one of the finest Italian restaurants in New York—our favorite cuisine. After stuffing ourselves, we took a slow, scenic walk down the lane. The streetlights were dim, casting a warm glow over the city. She gave me a concerned look, hinting that maybe we should take a cab and head home, but I insisted we keep walking a bit longer.

As we approached Midtown, the surrounding lights brightened, and suddenly, a string quartet began to play. "This is it," I thought to myself. I took a deep breath, went down on one knee, and pulled out the ring.

"Will you marry me?" I whispered, my heart pounding in my chest.

Lily's eyes widened, and she started jumping up and down before I could even get back on my feet. There were tears in both of our eyes as she hugged me tightly and screamed, "YES!"

It was the most beautiful moment of my life. I wished I had someone there to capture it, but in that instant, nothing else mattered. It was everything I had ever hoped for, and more.

Both of our families had known I was planning to propose, so when we called the next day to share the news, everyone was thrilled. It was such an exciting time for all of us. Six months later, we got engaged, and after a couple of years, we finally tied the knot. The wedding was a small, intimate ceremony—short, sweet, and full of joy. Everyone was laughing, smiling, and dancing the night away.

At first, we lived in Lily's apartment, but we had dreams of moving away from the city. We were saving up for a house, a place that we could truly call our own. Work was less hectic by then, as both of us had reached more comfortable positions after years of growing in the same firm. With senior roles came added responsibility, but also a sense of control and relaxation. Plus, the higher pay didn't hurt. Weekends were often ours to enjoy together, a reward for all the long hours we had put in. She was my partner in crime for everything.

We were both huge foodies, always eager to try something new. Mexican, French, Japanese, Italian, Indian—you name it, we tried it. We were especially fond of meat and seafood, sometimes venturing into the wildest of culinary experiences. I still remember the time we tried octopus—never again! We had no idea what we were getting into, and we spent the rest of the night laughing at our own adventurous (and regrettable) choice.

Travel was another thing we loved, and we explored as much as we could. We spent long days discovering new cities, walking along the beaches, or diving into water activities. One vacation, we took a two-day trek not far from our city. The view from the top of the cliff was breathtaking, a vast stretch of green as far as the eye could see. It was one of those moments that makes you feel small, like you're just a tiny part of this huge, magnificent world. It made me reflect on life, how there seemed to be a greater force at work, orchestrating everything in ways we could never fully understand.

We stayed in touch with my old colleagues too. Benjamin, as always, was a close friend to both of us. We met up with him every couple of weeks, sharing stories and keeping the friendship alive. Time flew by, and soon enough, we had saved up enough to put down a solid deposit on a house. It would take us about 5-10 years to pay off the loan, but it felt like a dream finally coming true.

We moved to Scarsdale when I was 28, about two hours away from the hustle and bustle of the city. The countryside gave us the peace we'd been craving. I couldn't help but smile the first time I looked at our new house. The timber beige walls, the beautifully shaped roof, the sunlight bouncing off the windows—it was perfect. "A place that's truly our own," I thought, marvelling at how far we'd come.

A year later, our first child was born—a boy. There's nothing in this world as beautiful as holding your newborn baby for the first time. "All that I am, and all that I have is yours," I whispered to him, overwhelmed with love. He was so small, so quiet, and I felt an inexplicable sense of peace just staring at him. We brought him home, and soon after, we had a christening at my parents' place. We named him Aaron.

Lily and I were rookies at parenting, learning everything as we went along. Four years later, we welcomed our second child—a baby girl. She was everything we had ever wanted, and she had Lily's beautiful eyes. We named her Eve. The moment she grabbed my finger with her tiny hand, my heart felt like it might burst. There's nothing more precious than that moment when your baby holds onto you like you're their entire world. I'd do anything for them—anything to keep them safe.

Reading that paragraph, I couldn't help but smile.

CHAPTER 17

FAMILY

The years flew by in a blur, and life with two kids was a whirlwind of work, love, and challenges. Taking care of Aaron and Eve was an all-consuming task, especially when they were young. I remember the first time we dropped them off at playschool. Their tiny hands gripped ours so tightly, their eyes wide with fear and tears welling up. They didn't want to let go. Lily and I had to practically peel them off us, and the sight of them crying as we walked away was heart-breaking.

Once we both started working from home once a week, things became a bit more manageable, though it was still chaotic. Between work, onsite visits, and taking care of the kids, our lives were a balancing act. There were nights when we didn't sleep at all, running on fumes and coffee as we took care of the babies. The house was a mess, baby toys and supplies scattered everywhere, and we'd baby-proofed every inch of the apartment to keep them safe. At times, it felt like we were running a circus, not a household.

The lack of sleep and the constant chaos bled into our work life. We argued a lot in those early days, frustrated by the lack of time for ourselves. But as time passed, we found a rhythm. We divided up the responsibilities and slowly learned to juggle everything. The one thing that got us through the toughest days was seeing our kids sleep peacefully, their little faces soft and serene. It was like magic—watching them sleep made all the stress and exhaustion worth it. It was our therapy, a reminder that despite the craziness, we were blessed with the greatest gift of all.

"Okay... this house sounds exactly like ours," I thought, feeling a strange sense of déjà vu.

I couldn't shake my curiosity. For days, I kept asking Mom questions, pestering her about Dad's past and our family history. Finally, one afternoon, as I was lounging in front of the TV, she brought out a large, old trunk. "Here are your answers," she said with a playful smile.

I opened it, and the first thing that hit me was a thick cloud of dust, making me sneeze. Inside were countless photographs and a giant scrapbook. The title read College Years, and I immediately flipped through the pages. "Oh my God," I gasped. Dad looked so young, with jet-black hair that was stylishly combed in every photo.

The pages were filled with memories—pictures of Dad and his friends in the dorm, sharing food, giving each other birthday bumps, eating at restaurants, and partying. There were even photos of them passed out after long nights. And sure enough, Uncle James was in almost every shot, grinning from ear to ear.

As I turned to the next page, I stopped cold. It was the iconic photo I had read about in the book—the game-winning shot, with Dad mid-air, the basketball in his hand, and the crowd on its feet. Goosebumps spread across my arms as I realized just how real these stories were. The next photo showed the team celebrating, lifting the trophy, confetti falling from the ceiling, their faces beaming with joy.

At the end of the scrapbook was a portrait of Mom. She was sitting in what looked like a cafeteria, her hair cascading down in waves, her eyes twinkling as she smiled at the camera. She looked exactly as I'd imagined the girl from Dad's story. The resemblance was uncanny, almost as if the description had been pulled from this very photograph.

There were more pictures scattered around the trunk—Mom and Dad together, goofing around, half of their faces covered by waffles, laughing at some inside joke. There were photos of family trips, weddings, and one especially cute picture of a chubby little boy, holding a piece of chocolate cake with wide, gleaming eyes.

"Wait… is this Dad?" I squinted at the photo. I couldn't believe it. The mischievous little boy in the picture was none other than my father. After sharing a laugh with Mom, I put the photos back, a new appreciation for these memories swirling in my mind and continued reading.

When Aaron was ten and Eve six, Lily and I decided it was time for their first theme park experience. The kids had been bouncing off the walls all week, excitedly counting down the days. It was the middle of summer vacation, and since Lily and I had a few days off, we figured it was the perfect time for a fun family day out.

"Alright, everyone ready?" I called out as we packed the last of the bags into the car.

Lily had, of course, prepared her signature healthy sandwiches for the trip.

"You sure you don't want a slice of pizza instead?" I teased, knowing how much of a health freak she could be.

She shot me a mock glare. "We'll see about that later," she said with a wink.

With sunscreen, towels, extra clothes, and everything else packed, we loaded into the car and set off for Wonderloom. As we pulled up, the giant, bold letters announcing the park loomed ahead, and Aaron and Eve could hardly contain their excitement.

"Wonderloom!" Aaron squealed. "Finally, we're here!"

It seemed we weren't the only family with this bright idea; the parking lot was packed, and families were everywhere.

"Looks like half the city had the same thought," I said, glancing at the long entrance line.

"Patience, love," Lily chuckled. "We'll get in."

After some waiting, we were finally inside the park. It was massive, so thankfully, the crowd split off toward different areas. The weather was just right—a sunny day with a cool breeze, which was a blessing.

We headed straight to the water slides. They were kid-friendly, so we could all enjoy them together. "I'm going first!" Aaron shouted, practically vibrating with excitement.

"Alright, champ, go for it!" I laughed as he positioned himself at the top of the slide, his face determined as he eyed the dark tunnel ahead.

And with a loud whoosh, he was gone, his screams of joy echoing all the way down.

"Your turn, love," I said to Lily, who was next in line. She gave a little smirk and, as usual, went down calm and collected.

Then, it was Eve's turn. She looked a little hesitant, biting her lip and glancing nervously down the slide. I crouched down beside her.

"Hey, kiddo, don't worry. It's gonna be a blast," I said reassuringly. "Just scream, laugh, and enjoy it. I'm right behind you, okay?"

Eve took a deep breath, her face relaxing a little. She nodded, lay down on the slide, and with one final look back at me, she was off. I heard her laughter echo as she twisted and turned down the tunnel.

"That's my girl," I thought as I followed right behind.

The cold water hit me with a splash at the bottom, and when I got out, I saw Lily,

Aaron, and Eve, all drenched, standing on the side, grinning from ear to ear.

"Well?" I asked, shaking off the water. "Who's ready for more?"

The kids' eyes lit up. "Let's do it again!" Aaron cried, and from there, we hopped from ride to ride, sliding down the water tubes, spinning on the lazy river, and even venturing into a dinosaur-themed boat ride that ended with a massive drop into a pool of water.

The boat ride was intense. As we climbed the long rail to the top, Eve squeezed my hand tightly, her eyes wide as we looked down at the water far below.

"You ready, champ?" I asked, grinning at Aaron.

"Let's do this!" he shouted, hyped up as usual.

And then, we were off—screaming as we hurtled down the slope and hit the water with a huge splash. Water flew everywhere, drenching us from head to toe. We stumbled out, shivering from the cold, but laughing hysterically.

"Wow, what a ride!" Lily said, wringing out her hair. "That was something."

By late afternoon, we were exhausted but still running on excitement. We took a break for drinks—cola for me and juice for the kids—before squeezing in a few more rides. Our final stop was the lazy river.

"Time to relax," I said, settling into the tube with Aaron on my lap. Lily and Eve floated by our side, peacefully drifting with the current.

"I could get used to this," Lily sighed.

After the lazy river, we were all too tired to go on. We showered, changed into warm clothes, and decided to call it a day. The kids, for once, agreed—they were wiped out.

"Alright, where to for dinner?" I asked as we piled into the car.

"Pizza!" Aaron and Eve shouted in unison.

Lily raised an eyebrow at me, and I couldn't help but chuckle. "I guess your sandwiches will have to wait," I teased.

We pulled into a nearby Domino's and feasted on pizza, the perfect end to a perfect day. None of us said much as we devoured our food, too hungry and tired to talk. By the time we got home, the kids were already half-asleep, and within minutes of hitting the pillows, we were all out cold.

As I drifted off, I couldn't believe how quickly time was flying. It felt like only yesterday we were dropping them off at playschool, and now they were 12 and 16. Life was moving fast, but days like this reminded me to soak up every moment.

CHAPTER 18

THE ESSENCE OF LIFE

Helping my parents retire was one of the proudest and most fulfilling moments of my life. I can still picture that conversation vividly—it brought tears to their eyes, and it's a memory I'll cherish forever. From the moment I started working at Walthouse Design, back when I was living with Benjamin and barely scraping by, I knew I wanted to give something back to them. It wasn't easy. For the first few years, I lived paycheck to paycheck. Every expense was carefully planned, every luxury postponed. But eventually, I managed to save a reasonable amount, enough to begin setting aside a portion for them.

It wasn't something they ever asked for. They probably didn't even need it. But I needed to do it. They had worked tirelessly their whole lives to provide me with the best of everything, often sacrificing their own comforts. For so long, I hadn't realized that, and I took it all for granted. This was my way of repaying them, of easing their burden and giving them the chance to slow down and enjoy life more comfortably. I knew they weren't getting any younger.

Last weekend, we celebrated my mom's 55th birthday.

It was a lively, heartwarming event with about fifty people in attendance—cousins, friends, family, all gathered in one place. There was music, party games, children running around, and the kind of laughter that fills a room and makes you feel at home. I could see how happy my parents were, and that sight alone made everything worth it.

Lily, the kids, and I had decided to stay with them for a week after the party. When the last of the guests had left and the house quieted down, I slipped into their room and handed them an envelope—a chunk of my savings that I knew would be more than enough for them to live out the rest of their lives comfortably.

I'll never forget the look on their faces. At first, they couldn't believe it, and then the tears came. My mom cried, my dad cried, and the three of us stood there in that small, intimate moment, overwhelmed with emotion. I hugged them both tightly, whispering, "It's time to relax now. Take some time for yourselves. You've earned it." Lily stood beside me, smiling through her own tears, and we all shared that moment of peace and gratitude together. Afterward, we celebrated in the simplest way possible—by making pancakes, drinking coffee, and watching Kung Fu Panda.

A month later, we did the same thing with Lily's parents. They were equally overwhelmed and hesitant to accept it at first. It took a lot of convincing, but eventually, they did. I could see the relief in their eyes, the gratitude.

Looking back, I feel like I'm living the happiest chapter of my life. From those early college days to the challenges of my first job, to marrying the love of my life and settling down, every step has been filled with its own lessons and rewards. I'm grateful for every single moment, and yet, I can't help but feel excited about what's to come.

And with that, I reached the end of the book. I gently closed it, taking a deep breath as the last word, "me...," echoed in my mind, leaving six dots hanging in the air. It felt like an invitation to reflect. I could see the entire journey replay in my mind—scene by scene, emotion by emotion. What a beautifully written story. I sat still for a few moments, replaying some of those key scenes in my head, savoring the experience.

I glanced over at Jason, who was buried in his comforter, only a small part of his face peeking out from between the pillows. He looked so peaceful. I made a mental note to get him to read this book. He wasn't much of a reader, but maybe this one would resonate with him. It certainly had with me.

The cold crept in from outside, and despite the heater working hard, I could still feel the chill. I got up, ducking beneath the curtains and peering out the window. The world outside was pitch dark, blanketed by softly falling snow. I pressed my hand against the icy glass, watching the wind whistle through the trees. Everything seemed still, peaceful, except for the snow quietly accumulating on the ground.

I couldn't help but hope that school would be cancelled tomorrow because of the weather. But then I remembered—the dance recital.

I could still feel the rush from last night—the way my imagination had run wild as I immersed myself in the book. Every scene played out so vividly in my mind. I could feel the fear of running through that thick forest, hearing the tiger's heavy footsteps approaching, its menacing face near the lake as I sprinted for my life. I could still picture that horrifying moment when the character looked in the mirror and saw the life-sized spider staring back at him, with its grotesque tentacles and scales. The image of the golden-tailed fish flopping helplessly in the fishbowl, its tiny world tainted by disgusting floating poop, stayed with me.

And then there was the fly—the one with only 24 hours to live. How those hours became the most meaningful of its life, even though it knew the end was near. I scanned through those parts quickly, as they were both intriguing and unsettling.

But amidst all those thoughts, one thing was clear: if I didn't get up tomorrow for my dance recital, mom was going to be furious. She had put in so much effort staying back with me for extra practice sessions, polishing every move with me. I couldn't let her down.

Lost in my musings, I didn't even notice the time. Suddenly, the door creaked open, and there stood dad—half-asleep, half-annoyed. He squinted at me, then at the clock, and finally at the open book lying across my bed. His expression softened as he spotted the pages. "You naughty little girl," he said with a soft chuckle. "Where did you find this?"

Without missing a beat, I launched into how much I loved the book, how it was a perfect blend of thriller and heart, how brilliantly dad had woven everything together. "Dad, this book is different. It's special," I gushed, barely pausing to breathe. "Is everything in it real? Did you really meet mom like that? Did uncle Benjamin really save you from the guard? And why all these characters—covering every species? Everything feels so familiar. Grandma's birthday, the house, the waterpark, even your job... it's all in here!"

He smiled warmly, clearly amused by my excitement. But then, with a glance at the clock, his tone shifted. "Don't you have a performance tomorrow at nine? It's already past midnight. Get some sleep, Belle. We'll talk tomorrow." He shut the door gently behind him, leaving me with a million unanswered questions swirling in my head.

Despite the excitement, I knew he was right. I had to wake up early. Somehow, I managed to drift off to sleep, though the book and dad's words still lingered in my mind.

The next morning, I woke up feeling a bit groggy, but the thrill of the recital quickly snapped me out of it. I arrived at the venue an hour early, my nerves building as we got ready in our costumes. The familiar flutter of anxiety and excitement buzzed in my stomach as the red curtain slowly opened. The packed auditorium unfolded before me, and in the crowd, I spotted familiar faces—mom and dad beaming with pride, Jason with his camera, Susan, Camille, and their parents waving with flowers in hand.

The music started, and the performance began. The adrenaline surged through me as I hit every move, every note, perfectly. I was lost in the dance, completely in tune with the music and my fellow dancers. The performance, based on *The Nutcracker*, felt magical. I danced as if I were in a dream, every step flawless, every emotion pouring out with grace.

As the final note echoed and the red curtain closed, the audience erupted into cheers. We held our final pose, basking in the applause. When the curtain finally fell, all of us dancers squealed in excitement, hugging each other tightly. It was perfect. We had nailed it.

I ran to my family after changing. They were waiting with open arms. Mom and dad showered me with praise, and Susan and Camille handed me the flowers they had brought. Jason, ever the teasing older brother, gave me a tight hug and said, "Good job, kiddo."

Dad suggested we celebrate with hot pretzels, and I couldn't agree more. We walked toward a nearby pretzel stand, and I clung to dad's hand, still buzzing from the performance.

As we waited for the pretzels, I glanced at dad with a look he knew all too well. "Not now, Belle," he said, laughing softly. But I couldn't help myself. "Just one thing... is the story finished?" I asked, eager for an answer.

He looked at me, then across the street as he started to walk. He paused, turned back with a grin, and said, "Who knows, cause this life isn't over yet!!"

"Hey, kiddo, don't worry. It's gonna be a blast," I said reassuringly. "Just scream, laugh, and enjoy it. I'm right behind you, okay?"

That's the essence of life….

THE END